The Grog Invasion

Best wishes
Griswald

The Grog Invasion

CHRONICLES OF THE LLANDODDIES

— as told by —

Griswallt ap Llechitwyt

y Lolfa

To wee folk everywhere, who keep sane those troubled by an insane world

First impression: 2006
Second impression: 2008

© Griswallt ap Llechitwyt and Y Lolfa Cyf., 2006

ISBN: 0 86243 892 6

Printed on acid-free and partly recycled paper
and published and bound in Wales by
Y Lolfa Cyf., Talybont, Ceredigion SY24 5AP
e-mail ylolfa@ylolfa.com
website www.ylolfa.com
tel (01970) 832 304
fax 832 782

Contents

see the Llandoddies website:

www.llandoddies.com

Llandoddieland c.1908

The character on the right is Hamish McSporran, one of the Dwarves of Disserth, who walked all the way from Scotland many years ago.

N
W E

SCALE: The pictorial projection of Llandoddieland is not to scale, and the system of **Geomorphic Elastification** has been used to include features which are actually many miles outside the perimeter of the area shown, such as Dôl-y-fan on the western edge. See also that Shaky Bridge has been slightly pushed down-river to afford an improved view. By employing **Supragnomic Perpective**, which was invented by the Gnomes of Nant-y-Grog, features on the Llandoddie scale have been incorporated into the human dimension. This applies to Plas Llanmorg and the Pustuled Toadstool Forest, among other features.

Seven Sisters of Dol-y-fan

River Ithon

River Ithon

Alpine Bridge

Llandrindod Wells

Bongam Bank

St Michael's Church Cefnlly

Cwm Coblyn

Un Shoor Tribe

Rock Park

Pump House Hotel

HQ Elfael Field Force

Shaky Bridge

Lover's Leap

Aberddd

Pustuled Toadstools

Ynysdod

Elves, Goblins & Smelly Rustics

Llandrindod Lake

Plas Llanmorg

Pentrosfa Mire

Blaenddgm

Llandrindod Hall

Llandoley

Dwarves of Disserth

Donkey track Hereford & London

o Builth Wells

Howey

Trolls

Cave

Acknowledgements

This book would never have seen the light of day had it not been for the bravery and enthusiasm of Michiel Blees: whilst all others who witnessed the antics of the Llandoddies kept a low profile, in case they were considered mad, prone to delusion under the influence of alchohol, or a strong case for the institution, Michiel worked hard to ensure that both the Doddies and the true history of Llandod were properly recorded. Both Catrin ap Lechitwyt and Brunhilde Kloptickler offered invaluable suggestions for improving accuracy of the accounts, and thanks must go to Melissa Blees for putting up with so many strange grown-ups. We would also like to acknowledge the kind help received from Alan Cunningham of Erwood Station Crafts' Centre, The Llandrindod Wells Spa Town Trust, The Mid-Wales Journal and Pete Jenkins of the Post Office, Llandrindod.

AUTHOR PROFILE

Very much a recluse, **Griswallt ap Llechitwyt** has written numerous books, and is a recognised authority on the Llandoddies of Llandrindod Wells. He has compiled a record of their many exploits, from the various writings of several scholars of Doddie culture, one or two of whom claim to have conversed with the little folk. Others have handed down their knowledge by word of mouth and, of course, there are Llechitwyt's own observations of the Llandoddies, made over a great many years. These observations have also enabled him to draw accurate portraits of these fascinating people, to illuminate the text.

Llechitwyt dislikes crowds and, at times, can be extremely rude to those who seek him out, so he is generally best left well alone. He is normally to be seen carrying a bag of smelly rabbits and a long staff.

It is advised that anyone under the age of 18 who reads this book should be accompanied by a responsible adult not given to fits, giggling and eruptions of the wind.

Background Notes on Llandoddies

It is said that the origins of Llandoddies go back into the mists of time, long before even the Mabinogion, though it is impossible to state with absolute confidence which of the many variations on Doddie evolution is correct. Some sources attribute most prominence to the Legend of the Chalybeate Spring theory, a more recent event, whereby, one day in the 1740s, Griffith Llyncrapper, keeper of the Chalybeate Spring in the Rock Park, failed to come home after work. Some time later, one moonlit night, a tiny figure was seen gliding down the Ithon, astride a small twig. The figure appeared to be less than three inches in height, and Old Thomas, who was out fishing, saw it and reckoned it was the spitting image of Griffith Llyncrapper. Had he shrunk so drastically? If so, how had it happened? Later, other little folk were occasionally seen, sometimes with Griffith. Over the years, it became noticed that others who worked at the spring also disappeared. Sometimes, the disappearance occurred during the visit of a tall stranger, who rode a jet-black mare, but some reckoned there was magic at work. Whatever the cause, it was never satisfactorily explained.

Griffith, before his disappearance, had many arguments with those in authority and was known to be extremely angry about the way the community was run. It is likely that if, indeed, it was he who had turned into a 'little person', he would have wanted to keep some distance between himself and the humans, or Grumpies, as the Doddies called them. It is, therefore, logical that Doddies do not wish to have contact with the strange ways of Grumpies, although many reckon there is a more sinister reason.

Doddie Settlements

Doddies still work at the springs, checking the quality of the mineral water, keeping the water clear of rubbish, and ensuring that it is the right colour. Each day they test its wetness by throwing a bucket of water over Will Pant-y-felin, the water-tester. The increase in Grumpie activity in Llandrindod has forced many to look elsewhere, and though some stayed, most Doddies settled at Aberdod, where the Afon Dod, a Doddie name, runs into the north shore of the lake. Aberdod was hidden amongst undergrowth, away from prying eyes. Later, a hedge was planted around the site. Many

Doddies thought this was a deliberate act of kindness by some friendly Grumpie.

Aberdod expanded into a large village; the Doddies mainly set up homes under tree roots, in abandoned nests and warrens, hollow trees or thick bushes. These were turned into extremely comfortable dwellings, the occupants taking advantage of Grumpie cast-offs such as broken glass, metal, etc, which they ingeniously recycled for their own use. Each dwelling is as close to a water source as possible, and they are all adept at capturing rainwater. Some of the more affluent Doddies actually built homes of stone and human cast-offs, but these had to be carefully sited so as not to be visible to Grumpies. When the road was built round the lake, most Doddies transferred all their homes on to the island in the middle of the lake, and Doddie engineers worked hard to extend the underground railway to the island, travelling far under water, an amazing feat for such little folk. Their new settlement on the island is called Ynysdod.

Doddie Females

Female Llandoddies usually wear black hats with a plant or flower stuck in the ribbon: the addition of sphagnum moss indicates she is in love; a daffodil means she is married; gorse that she is confused; daisy, single; primrose, divorced but optimistic; a snowdrop means she is cold and in need of a *cutch* (cuddle).

The Grog invasion took place on St Cewydd's Day, 15th July 1908, when most Doddies lived at, or near, Aberdod, during the golden era of Llandrindod Wells spa.

Mrs Squnch

1. Proggie's Prognosis

FLYING HIGH above Llandrindod Lake, in perfect formation, the evening duck patrol cut through the grey, overcast sky, scanning the vista below for any tasty morsels that might present themselves. Suddenly, the starboard wing-man yelped in excitement.

"Doddie craft to starboard!"

"OK, Number Two, I see them," came the crisp, measured reply from his leader, Big Boy Bertie, out in front. "Triple-B Squadron, prepare to attack. Straighten up there, Matilda! Stand by to manoeuvre into attack formation."

Well used to descending on unsuspecting prey, Bertie adjusted course slightly and checked his squadron. Yes, the other four ducks flew behind him, in immaculate arrow-head formation, awaiting his command. Bertie enjoyed these moments most of all: the thrill of excitement at the start of the dive and the knowledge that the whole formation hung on to his every word.

"Let them wait a few more moments, while I bask in the coming glory." thought Bertie.

"*Tally-ho!*" he cried, immediately peeling off to the right and beginning a long, shallow dive, with the others following in perfect line astern. "Follow me, chaps."

"Bighead!" grumbled Matilda, who brought up the rear. She had no stomach for chasing the little Doddies behind this bigoted old fowl, and knew full well what the outcome would be. She'd seen it many times before.

The patrol arced in a wide, curving dive, relying on their leader to land as close to the target as possible and surprise their prey. Ducks, however, are not amongst the best tacticians. The long, winding approach ahead of the Doddie craft gave the Doddies ample time to become alert to the threat. Big Boy Bertie banked to the right and lined up on the target, skimming low above the water, but still having to pull hard to starboard during the final approach. The slight miscalculation was enough to cause him to overshoot. He hit the water with a terrific splash. Closely following, his starboard wing-man momentarily took his eye off his leader, to check the position of the target, just as he was about to land. Like Bertie, he overshot, and the distraction caused him to crash into his leader with an almighty thump, which sent them both cart wheeling over the surface of the water.

The next two ducks belly-flopped in behind them, causing mayhem, but Matilda, having spotted the chaos, had time to adjust, and she flew over the sad group as they thrashed about. She turned round and calmly landed nearby, looking decidedly superior, while her friends sorted themselves out. By the time the ducks had regrouped into proper formation, there was no sign of the Doddie boat. A strange, low mist hung over the water where the craft had been.

"Anyone seen the boat?" asked Matilda, smirking in the knowledge that she had been proved right once again. The Llandoddies were too smart by far.

"We must have sunk them when we shot past," replied Bertie, looking rather cross, and certainly not wanting to admit that he didn't have a clue. "Let's get airborne and see if we can find something else."

The three-Doddie coracle glided effortlessly across the calm water, shielded by the low mist, while its occupants flung baked newt-bladder crystals into the surrounding water to create a fine cloud that rose from the surface of the lake. This mingled with the soft drizzle and hid them from the duck patrol that they had spotted at the start of its diving attack. The coracle, with its dragon-head prow, pottered along slowly, propelled by the Doddies' webbed feet. The craft had three pairs of holes in the bottom, through which the crew members passed their legs. Doddie legs fitted snugly into the holes; their rubbery skin prevented any water from entering the craft.

"I think the ducks have given up," said the small fellow sitting in the middle. "We can relax now."

His larger companion nodded in agreement. Ducks, though ungainly fighters, could savage Doddies in their beaks and leave them crippled. They did not always attack, but when they did, it was frightening; and why they did was a complete mystery to the Doddies.

Little Dewi, or Dewi Bach, had known his friend, Big Dewi, since they went to Aberdod school together, so they worked with a harmony that many envied. Well, at least, Little Dewi worked in harmony: Big Dewi, or Dewi Mawr, was a bit too big and awkward, and more inclined to use his brains to hammer in a fencepost than for thinking things out. After all, there are some advantages to having a forehead like a sledgehammer. Although something of a buffoon, he was well-loved by others, especially by Wild Blodwen, who flirted with him at every opportunity. Alas, being slow on the uptake, he was utterly confused by her amorous advances. Big Dewi lived alone, but his Mam sent food parcels to his tree.

Even though he was 42 years old, which is fairly young for a Doddie, Little Dewi still lived with his parents. Doddies are said to live for about 265 years, due to their healthy outdoor life and laid-back attitude. Little Dewi was much fancied by Martha Stiffjog, the games mistress, although her amazing energy left him breathless. He hadn't yet got round to actually kissing her. He really had a fond eye for Daisy Davies, who ran evening classes in flower arranging, but, somehow, he just could not summon up the courage to take up flower arranging, especially as the class was made up solely of females.

The third occupant of the coracle, Esmerelda, affectionately known as Essie, had grown up with the two Dewis, but she didn't seem interested in boys. While most Doddie females tended to be rather portly, Essie was less so, and was regarded as one of the lads. She could easily keep up with them, when they were out walking, and she worked as assistant to Little Dewi, who was a snufter's assistant. Like her cousin Martha, she was the grand-daughter of Myfanwy, who had had a romantic fling with Bad Idwal, the Elf. This liaison accounted for the elfin appearance of the two girls. Both wore short, elf-like skirts, which were considered rather risqué for late Victorian times. In fact, Mrs Maudlin-Grommet protested vigorously about Martha's exposure of flesh, and would not allow her girls to attend games lessons taught by 'such a floosie.' Essie had ambitions to get into the Aberdod ibgur team, but because there were only five places in the ladies' team, she was up against stiff competition.

The trio had been out fishing for two days, but had caught nothing. The hot summer seemed to be affecting the fish badly, and, as Doddies love their fish more than anything else, it caused concern, especially as Big Dewi relied on catching fish for his business, which was the making of fish cakes and all manner of fishy products. The onset of the rain, however, cheered them up, as the fish were now more likely to bite. This felt like heaven to the Doddies, for they appreciated nothing better than a light dowsing, being the water-folk of Llandod. As they moved across the water, they drew along their nets, occasionally pulling them in, to see if anything had been caught. At times, they stopped paddling and threw out fishing lines; then, they relaxed or snoozed at leisure. As the soft rain began to moisten them, the trio broke into song, as Doddies often do at any opportunity. Strains of the *Ithon Waggling Song* drifted across the water:

"Jolly good waggling weather
a downpour in Llandod.
We waggle along the Ithon,
And really don't give a sod

Crash-landing of Big Boy Bertie and his duck squadron

If we're wetter than a haddock
Or slippery as a cod,
We'll all waggle together
On our way home to Llandod"

Although this was traditionally sung on the River Ithon, it was equally popular with Doddies in a coracle on Llandod Lake. The singing trailed off; in the quiet that followed, Little Dewi's thoughts drifted back to their departure from Aberdod, on the north shore of the lake. The Prognosticator had begged them not to go out on the water.

"Woe!" he had moaned with great emotion. "The signs are verr-rr-ry bad – don't go fishing… beware the swamp ho- ho- horr-rdes. Oh, Woe! Beware the queen – she stings harr-rr-dest."

"What d'you think old Proggie meant by telling us to beware the swamp hordes, beware the queen?" Little Dewi piped up.

"No idea," said Essie, "but there's passionate, he was. I wish he didn't talk in riddles all the time."

"I don't think he knows what he's talking about half the time. Anyway, it's all above my head," said Big Dewi ponderously. "I thought he'd really clagged his faffer, when he started on about cakes waving in the breeze, and then going into his mystical chanting, and stomping around like some woolly-brained witch-doctor. And, then, he mentioned something about watching the vessel with care."

"He must have meant our boat. The old fool's half-mad," said Little Dewi, lazily flopping his hand in the water. "Shall we start for home now, and camp in a while, then continue to Aberdod tomorrow, is it?"

He changed the subject. The bizarre behaviour of the Prognosticator was way beyond the comprehension of most Doddies.

"Well, I know we haven't caught anything and we were almost pulled into the water by that eel, but I do love being out here," replied his big friend. "With this rain, I think we should stay out another day, and see if we can catch something. Bit embarrassing, it is, to go home with an empty sponger."

Here, on the southern end of the lake, was a long way from home for a Doddie boat to be paddled. Doddies, on average, are only two and three-eighth inches high, although Big Dewi rose to the towering height of two and fifteen-sixteenths inches.

Little Dewi agreed, but Essie scowled. She'd had enough of this fishing expedition and wanted to get back to Aberdod in time for St Cewydd's Festival, due to take place tomorrow. Being the patron saint of rain, St Cewydd was much revered by Doddies.

"I think we should head straight back at once," she said, "or we'll miss the festivities, and, anyway, I'm bored." Having been cramped for so long in a coracle the size of a kipper-dish, she needed to get back on land.

"Even if we head for home now, we won't be back in time for the start," interrupted Little Dewi.

"That's a feeble excuse. What you mean to say is, you men aren't up to waggling to Aberdod in a short time. You are so sad."

Essie tore into the lads, as she often did

when she thought they were ganging up on her. She waved her arms aggressively at the other two, rising partly out of her seat at the same time.

"Sit you down, *bach*," said Little Dewi, "or you'll have us all in the water." He found females difficult, when they became emotional.

As they came into sight of the rocky headland known as *Trwyn-y-wrach,* Little Dewi signalled to his friends to slow down.

"Gentle you go, now. We don't want to hit the sharp rocks under the surface, so don't go dull for a moment or two, Dewi," he yelled, anticipating possible hazards that might be caused by his friend's erratic movements as he thrust his feet into maximum braking position. "There's a lovely campsite round the headland, in Trellyfan Bay (Toadstown), where we can stay tonight."

"Can you smell something horrible?" Essie wrinkled up her nose.

"Dewi. Can you explain that awful smell?" asked Little Dewi, half grinning.

Big Dewi grunted dismissively and ignored the remarks. The coracle floated past the rocky headland.

"This is the life – not a care in the world. You can expect a tug on the line at any moment."

Little Dewi admired the shapes of the rocks, as they glided past the headland. The Doddies were sitting with their backs to the prow, little realising the danger they were drifting into.

"You're just changing the subject," argued Essie, scowling at her companions. "We should be getting back home. We're running out of food and I'm fed up with catching nothing, and sitting around all day. Gosh! What's that noise?" Essie asked, interrupting herself. Sounds of activity made them turn to see what was happening.

"Ow!" exclaimed Essie, trying to stifle a yell.

Big Dewi instantly looked over his shoulder, which caused the craft to roll alarmingly to starboard. He started in fright, unable to believe what his eyes saw. Expecting a calm, peaceful bay, they were confronted by a seething mass of activity that stretched along the shoreline for as far as they could see into the misty murk. Beached on the muddy shore were countless craft, mostly of a warlike type, though there seemed to be a number of fishing-boats amongst them. Strange, half-reptile, half-gnome figures scurried about. They were larger and darker than Doddies.

"Grogs!" breathed Little Dewi, his face drained of colour.

Even Big Dewi shivered at the prospect of meeting this warrior race from the Carneddau Hills. They were the traditional enemies of the Doddies, and several vicious confrontations had happened over the years. The coracle was well out from the rocks and easily visible from the shore. They tried to turn the craft round and head away from this exposed position, but the coracle would not respond properly.

"Essie's fainted," yelled Little Dewi. "Her feet are dragging in the water, and she's slumped over on one side. It's hard to steer."

"Throw some water in her face."

While Little Dewi revived Essie, his friend made hard work of turning the coracle, which had drifted closer to the Grogs, who were busy taking things ashore from their boats. The fishy smell that came drifting across from them appalled the Doddies. They could be spotted at any moment, while in such an exposed place. It only needed one Grog to look up and spot them. After Dewi had saturated Essie's face, she started to come round, spluttering and indignant that Dewi was giving her such a wetting. Slowly, the coracle turned its prow back towards *Trwyn-y-wrach*.

The friends realised that, nimble as their coracle was, it could not compete with the speed of the Grog war boats. Had they been spotted? Their little legs waggled furiously back towards *Trwyn-y-wrach,* as they kept their eyes on the Grog movements. Only when they passed the headland once more and were rapidly being swallowed up in the mist did they relax. It seemed that the Grogs had been too intent on their work to have noticed the Doddie craft. The misty drizzle became a saviour.

"Better go back home straight away," said Big Dewi, choking out the words in his excitement. It was unusual to see the big fellow so disturbed.

"Dewi, we've had a long, hard day of paddling and fishing," replied his little companion. "It will take a day's waggling to get home, and I'm fair dulled with exhaustion. No, we must find out what them Grogs are doing. They're not just on a fishing trip, not with all those war boats. Something funny is going on. Let's land under the trees further along, and creep along the shore after dark, to see if we can find out what they are up to. We certainly don't want to be out on the lake after dark, in case we get caught by the Spirits of the Lake."

The legendary Spirits of the Lake were said to be dark, hooded fiends that preyed on anyone foolish enough to be out on the lake at night.

"You're right," said Essie, recovering from her fainting fit. "Serious, it is, that's for sure. Now we know what old Proggie was going on about!" Despite her desire to get home to Aberdod, she realised that they needed to find out whether these warlike creatures might pose a threat. "But," she said firmly, "there's no way I'm going near them Grogs. You boys will have to find out what they are doing."

Doddie coracle on Llandrindod Lake

Big Dewi saw the sense in what his friends suggested. The Grogs had obviously not seen them, and so they silently drifted into the shelter of a rocky cove and sank the coracle in fairly shallow water, to be recovered later. Doddie coracles are designed to be left at the bottom of the lake, anchored down until needed, and invisible to anyone wandering by. While it was still light, they set up their simple moleskin shelters and made a delicious pot of Doddie tea. Smoke from the fire would not be seen in this mist, which had really closed in. Nevertheless, the trio took turns to watch for Grogs. The warm tea revived their spirits.

"I'm scared. I don't like them Grogs," croaked Big Dewi hoarsely, in low tones, as though he expected them to be listening nearby. "They're up to no good. I'm not going over there. I'll stay with Essie. We'll have to be careful; if they catch us, they'll feed us to the sewer-rats. It's worse than being attacked by a whole gaggle of ducks."

Doddies hated ducks. For some reason, their foul-smelling squirt-bags, so useful in putting a cat, dog or rat to flight, were ineffective against ducks.

"I don't want to go either," said Little Dewi, "but one of us must."

"If they see you, they'll easily catch you." Essie grimaced. "They are much faster than we are, and there's so many of them."

By now, Big Dewi was beside himself with fear. "What can we do? What will happen to Mam and Gwyneth if this horde attacks Aberdod? What about our friends? We must do something. Those Grogs have evil written all over them, and Aberdod is the only place they could be heading for, from here."

In the dim light, the two Dewis crept gingerly along the shoreline of Trellyfan Bay, taking pains not to make the slightest noise. Each was engrossed in his own thoughts and concentrating on not alerting the Grogs. Big Dewi, though terrified, had been persuaded to go along. Suddenly, they felt a bush move behind them. Big Dewi froze, the shock of fright shot up his spine, causing him to gasp in anticipation of an attack. A shadowy figure emerged from the bush and, just as Dewi was about to strike out, he realised it was Essie.

"What are you doing here? I thought you were staying behind. Fair frightened me, you did!"

"I was too terrified to stay on my own in the dark," whispered Essie, "so I'm coming with you."

The three continued along the shore. The Grogs had not posted any sentries. In fact, they were making a dreadful racket, as they laughed, belched and devoured raw meat, and took great delight in spitting mouthfuls of half-eaten food onto their neighbour's meat. The Doddies listened in trepidation, from behind a tent. After a while, an awesome giant of a Grog got to his feet and swaggered around the large fire, the light of the flames turning his features into grotesque shapes, and glistening on his sweaty torso. Close proximity to the Grogs made the three friends gasp in horror as they huddled together in the shadows. These repulsive creatures provoked fear and awe, with their cruel, reptilian heads, rows of bone-crushing teeth, muscular, scaly bodies and vile habits. They gorged themselves on small lake creatures, tearing them apart while they were still alive, and swilling them down with the potent, foul-smelling toad-juice that usually put them into a drunken stupor.

Aaaargh!" The roar from the giant seemed to vibrate the ground and echo across to the headland. He demanded attention from the horde. They fell silent.

"Tomorrow, we shall rip the Llandoddies apart," he barked, addressing the whole company, and raising a clenched fist as he did so. His audience croaked approvingly. "Eingart, you take the fishing boats home, while the rest of us sail to Aberdod. We'll beach the boats and attack the Doddies before they know what's hit them!"

"Oh no!" gasped Essie, wringing her hands in fear.

"Quiet, Essie," snapped Little Dewi in hushed tones, "or they'll hear us."

"Ongut, we should leave the boats anchored some way off and sneak up on the Doddies overland," said one of the older Grogs, who chewed a large piece of raw fish. "The main group can attack the Doddies, after they have had their afternoon tea and would…"

"*Afternoon tea?* Ah ha ha!" A huge Grog, who had been drinking by the fire, roared with laughter, his loud, rasping, mocking voice carried across the clearing to all assembled. "Is that what they do? We'll pulverise them into

their strawberries and cream. Ha ha ha!"

He sat, laughing at his own joke, until someone poured a bowl of lukewarm fish soup over him. Both Grogs rolled over and continued scrapping on the ground, until Ongut became fed up with the pair and smashed both on the head with a large club. Seeing him knock out both fighters, the rest went quiet again.

The Grog leader looked around, menacingly at his followers. He thrust out his chest, stretching his holey vest almost to breaking point, as the flickering firelight revealed his yellowy-green, scaly arms. Reaching down with one arm, he grabbed the neck of one of the prostrate Grogs, hauled him into the air above his head with both hands, and then brought the unfortunate creature down with such force that he broke its back on a sharp rock. The audience gasped in awe. Essie fainted and crashed to the ground. Luckily, nobody heard her fall because of the loud gasps. Ongut strode around like a bantam cock, revelling in his callous performance.

The two lads tried frantically to revive Essie.

"Kiss her better, Dewi."

"I'm not kissing her," grumbled Big Dewi. "Never kissed a girl in my life, and don't intend to, not ever!"

"I saw you kissing Blod the other day."

"No, she was kissing *me,* and I was trying to stop her."

Several minutes passed before Essie came round.

"After their tea, the Doddies will be sleepy. The main attack group will approach along the shore. The second group can take the rear, and capture their women and cakes, as well as all the valuables they can find. But it's their cakes that are the main target."

Ongut twitched after every sentence, a sign that he was working up to a fanatical pitch. His hooded right eye blinked like an anaconda forcibly digesting its prey. Doddie ladies were well-known for baking the most amazingly delicious cakes. By kidnapping them, the Grogs were guaranteed a continuous supply of cakes, which was their favourite food.

"Will they have lots of jellies and fairy cup-cakes?" growled a fierce looking Grog; he had Rastafarian dreadlocks half covering his scarred face. He sat sharpening his sword. "I love jellies."

A large female Grog rose to her feet and sauntered provocatively across to the fire. "I'll take on the Doddie ladies. We girls are dying for a scrap." Leila received a great cheer for her bravado, which encouraged her to be even more aggressive. She bristled with energy; the metal bands on her arms flashed in the firelight. "I'll make 'em crawl on all fours to our boats." she snarled, lashing a leather frog-whip across her ample thigh. One of the male Grogs made a playful lunge at her. She immediately kicked sand in his face, and, having momentarily blinded him, brought her whip down with a crash on his huge nose.

"Ha! Ha! Ha!" she laughed. He yelped like a puppy and backed off. "I can't wait for tomorrow."

Essie whimpered, when Leila strode towards their hiding place. Little Dewi thrust her into a bush for protection; Big Dewi was mesmerised at the sight of this brutish Grog female. Had she somehow sensed their presence?

"Get ready to run," whispered Little Dewi, knowing full well that it would be impossible for them to out-run these athletic creatures.

"You will stay and guard the boats, Leila," roared Ongut, scowling disdainfully at her. "It's because you females are so hopeless at cooking and baking that we have to raid the Doddies!"

Leila turned back, away from where the

Opposite: The Grog Camp

Doddies stood quaking in fear behind a bush, and swaggered up to Ongut, hands on hips and aggressively chewing an immature newt. She stood eyeball-to-eyeball with him, something which none of the other Grogs would dare to do. The trembling trio of Doddies backed further into the dark undergrowth.

"Try and stop me," Leila snarled, twisting her body like a cobra about to strike. "My girls will be in the thick of it."

She turned to face a large Grog, and spat the half-chewed newt into his scarred face. Ongut flinched. He debated whether to give Leila a good thrashing and put her in her place, but she was very fast and might well send him flying into the lake, as he had a clumsy way of moving. She could make a complete fool of him, with her superb athleticism. He backed off and turned to Igrun, pretending to lose interest in Leila.

"Igrun, you're in charge of the attack. Just make sure these females don't mess it up for us."

Igrun snorted and half-choked; he had been eating an enormous mouthful of something slimy that still squirmed, half inside his mouth. He belched, and the contents of his mouth spewed across the makeshift table and into several soup bowls. He spluttered, rose to his feet and crashed his huge fist down on the table.

"Urggh!" he sniffed noisily, "I'll sort out Leila later." He again belched, and sat down with a thump, to the laughs of his men.

Little Dewi grimaced. His head and shoulders were bowed in apprehension as they tip-toed back to their shelters. After some moments, he tried to speak, but his emotions got the better of him. Eventually, his words burst out in anger.

"We must get back to Aberdod straight away, to warn the others... otherwise, it will be a massacre."

"I'm exhausted," replied Big Dewi, chewing a piece of grass. "Anyway, we'd get lost in the dark, or meet the spirits. Let's get some rest now, and see what the morning brings."

"But, we must have a plan. It'll be too late in the morning. We can't let the others down," protested Essie, still dazed at Ongut's callous disregard for life.

"We could rise very early and set off as dawn is breaking."

"No, Dewi, we haven't got the speed of the Grog boats. They would rapidly overtake us. Why don't we climb up Pant-y-goggin gorge, and see if old Haydn the Hermit can help us?" Little Dewi had a high regard for the hermit.

"But, he's as old and decrepit as my

grandmother," argued Essie. "He spends his time making cabbage-ladders. How can he help?"

"I'm not sure, but he's our only hope. At least, he has a tame frog that one of us could ride, and he'd know the quickest way to get home overland. Let's set off early and climb up the gorge."

"You know, I feel that, even if we could get back home this instant and warn the whole of Aberdod, we still wouldn't be able to stop this lot. Whatever we do to defend ourselves, they'll overwhelm us. We'll have to evacuate Aberdod and everyone will have to hide in the hills." Essie paused. She was always quick to sum up people and situations. "But," she said, "we've got to try, for everyone's sake, so you two better had get your skates on in the morning."

Try as she would, Essie found it impossible to sleep. She lay awake, anxiously going over the day's events. She mused over Proggie's parting words: "Beware the queen – she stings harr-rr-dest," He must have meant that dreadful Leila, she decided. How Essie wanted to *cutch* up to the lads for comfort, but she knew they would be embarrassed. At times during that long night, she felt almost paralysed with fright and, in view of what she knew lay before them, she wished the morning would never come.

Dewi Mawr

2. The Chase

LONG BEFORE DAWN, Little Dewi arose; the night was still as black as the inside of Big Dewi's fish-sponger. He had had little sleep, having been constantly rocked by his companion's thunderous snoring, which sounded like intermittent volcanic eruptions. Little Dewi pulled on his coat and went to arouse the big lad. As he did so, Big Dewi suddenly exploded with an almighty snore, accompanied by a thrashing of arms and legs that hurled Little Dewi several feet into the air, and he landed on the backside of a sleeping hedgehog.

"Aargh!" yelled the little fellow, instantly realising that all Grogs within twenty miles must have heard the commotion.

"What's going on?" A sleepy voice came out of the darkness. Essie had woken up. Sensibly, she had slept some distance from Big Dewi, well aware of his amazing capacity to snore.

Big Dewi fell back into slumber as his friend picked himself up and was joined by Essie. Luckily, no sound came from the direction of the Grog camp. The big lad must be awakened quickly; every minute counted today.

"I've an idea," said Essie. She sidled up to where he lay and began gently stroking Big Dewi's enormous nose with a strand of long grass. Unfortunately, Big Dewi not only suffered from snoring, but also from hay-fever. Tickling him on the nose with grass was, to say the least, asking for trouble.

It took some time to arrive, but when it did, it was truly amazing. First, Big Dewi's nose twitched from right to left; at the same time, it seemed to glow and swell up like an over-active prut. His brow furrowed and his huge arms clawed the air. At the same time, his head swayed from side to side, his cavernous mouth opened, and he let out the loudest ear-splitting sneeze the others had ever heard. Unfortunately, Little Dewi again happened to be directly in the firing line. He shot across the grass, and landed head-first into a pile of rotting liverworts, into which he sank, groaning. The deep, gungy, smelly, wet muck did not improve his feeling of well-being one jot. Essie, summoning all her strength, dragged him out, with some difficulty, certain now that the Grogs had been alerted, for she could hear movement and sounds from the Grog camp.

"Get up, Dewi," urged Little Dewi, recovering from his battering. "You've gone dull on us again. The Grogs'll be upon us if we don't get out of here fast."

Alas, his words fell on deaf ears. Big Dewi, now once more fast asleep, appeared to be having quite a dream, as he rolled around and talked in his sleep. Little Dewi grabbed the big fellow's hat and filled it with marsh-water, which contained a considerable amount of mud. Taking careful aim, he threw it over his friend's face. Sadly for the luckless Big Dewi, in the water was a tiny marsh-crab, which quickly grasped his huge honk, causing the big lad to erupt with a howl of pain. Again, he lashed out, this time flinging Little Dewi into the uppermost spikes of a thistle, where he hung helplessly, while Big Dewi stamped the ground and roared like a bull, until he managed to wrench the crab off his nostril.

"Get me down," groaned Little Dewi. Essie ran over and quickly helped the little lad down from the thistle.

"Stop fooling around, Dewi. We must pack up and get going," she urged, gathering her things together. "The Grogs can't see us in the dark, but I can hear them moving. They'll be here any minute."

Big Dewi, having recovered, flung as much as he could into his enormous fish-sponger, which smelt like a fish market, as the sound of the approaching enemy drew nearer. Then, a sharp crashing of undergrowth nearby alerted them to Grogs almost upon them.

Rapidly-moving shadows flitted through the undergrowth. An enormous Grog, panting and snorting heavily, burst out of the tall grasses and floored Little Dewi with a blow. When the Grog grabbed his knife, intending to finish Dewi off, Big Dewi head-butted the attacker. The Grog crumpled in a heap; an encounter with Dewi's head was like being hit by a steamroller.

"Come on, there's more of them," whispered Essie urgently. They all leapt into the bushes and hid, trying to make out the Grogs in the complete darkness.

"Look," whispered Little Dewi, "there's Grogs by the shore. See them silhouetted against the lighter water? If we sneak away inland and move round to where the coracle is, we should escape. It'll be dark for some time yet."

The Doddies crept along parallel to the shoreline, trying not to betray their presence with any noise. Lights began to filter through the trees – some of the Grogs had brought torches along and were combing the undergrowth for the Doddies. In the dark, it

The Grog girls fall on Big Dewi as Essie tries to help

was difficult for the three friends to move fast, and the Grog line gained on them.

"Nearly there," said Little Dewi. "I'll go on ahead and get the coracle up from the bottom of the water."

He disappeared into the dark. Shortly afterwards, the others heard a faint splash, as Little Dewi entered the water and dived down to the coracle.

"Hope he's quick." Essie's heart was pounding with excitement as she clung to Big Dewi, while they crouched under a bush. "That torch is getting very close."

"I'll see if he needs a hand," said Big Dewi, embarrassed at being in such close contact with a female. He was rather afraid that Essie might hug him, a horrible female habit. He rose and walked a short distance to the water, scanning the surface for signs of his friend. Not a ripple stirred the water. It couldn't be easy to find the coracle in the dark.

Essie sat in the intense blackness, paralysed with fear, watching the torch come closer. She wondered what to do if she was found. Suddenly, the light of the torch was upon her. Shadowy figures closed in. Essie screamed, turned away and tried to squirm further into the thick bush.

"Look, Leila," croaked a rough female Grog voice from behind the torch, "there's a little girl-Doddie."

One of the others strode forward and grabbed Essie, bending her arm behind her back until she thought it was going to break. She was dragged to her feet by the tall Grog, and spun round to face her captor, the cruel features of Leila recognisable from the previous evening.

"Aha," grinned Leila. "So, little Doddie, I'll break your arms, unless you tell me where are your friends are."

She needn't have bothered; with a terrific crash, Big Dewi came through the vegetation like a marauding elephant, his sights on Leila, having heard Essie's scream. Alas, he didn't see the squat, thick-set Hannie in the dark. She stuck out her huge Grog foot. Dewi tripped over it and hit the ground with a breath-sapping thump. Leila flung Essie to one side and fell on top of Dewi. She thrust her knee on to the back of his neck, whilst Hannie grabbed his arms. Leila tried to drag her sword out of its scabbard but Essie held it back momentarily; but, for the Doddie lass, it was like a flea trying to wrestle a cart-horse. Dewi roared and rolled over, just as the third Grog female swung at him with a massive club. It missed and caught Hannie instead, knocking her out.

Leila threw Essie off and pulled out her sword, to carve Dewi into little pieces, as he dodged another blow from the club. Just as Leila was about to plunge it into Dewi, the irrepressible Essie jabbed her in the eye with a rolled-up copy of the Llandod Underground Railway Map and Summer Timetable. Temporarily blinded, Leila yelled in rage as Dewi punched her and managed to struggle free. The girl with the club backed off and shouted to the warriors to hurry up. Dewi grabbed Essie's hand and they ran into the lake, where Little Dewi had the coracle afloat. Essie took a flying leap into the coracle as Dewi began to take it into deeper water. He could just make out the Grog warriors racing into the lake behind Big Dewi, who fell into the water and began to swim.

Essie took out the middle pair of bungs and thrust her legs through the bottom of the boat as Big Dewi caught up with them.

"Stay in the water for a moment, Dewi," said Little Dewi. "Hang on to the boat and don't do anything dull. We'll pull you out to deep water, and then you can come in."

To stop for Dewi to climb in would have risked being caught, but as they pulled away, the Grogs could do nothing but hurl stones at them. Once out far enough from the shore, they stopped and, with great difficulty, hauled the big fellow into the light craft. A whale would hardly have made more fuss. Eventually, he was in position and they began to move again.

"Oh, no, the Grog boats are after us already!" Essie broke the calm as she pointed to two large boats rounding *Trwyn-y-wrach*. Their dark silhouettes set against the lighter water emphasised their evil profiles, and the air was filled with the sound of the Grog crews chanting.

"They didn't waste time," shivered Little Dewi. "But I don't think they can see us, because we're against the dark shoreline. We must get round the next headland and into the bay by the stream. There, we can sink the coracle again and follow the stream up the valley to Haydn's."

"But they'll see us as we round the end of *Craig-y-twiddle*."

"Nothing we can do about it. Waggle as hard as you can and keep going," Little Dewi had no intention of giving up. "Don't forget – rhythm – don't panic. We've got a good start on them."

Gradually, the Doddies worked their way to the edge of *Craig-y-twiddle* and, waggling for all they were worth, kept glancing at the danger that was fast approaching. Increased chanting from the Grog boats indicated that they had been spotted. The boats appeared much bigger now, the chanting more threatening, and the Grogs were beating on their shields.

The three friends kept their heads and slowly pulled into the far bay. They came temporarily out of sight of the Grogs, as the friendly bulk of *Craig-y-twiddle* intervened, though they could still hear the frightening chant of "Gra Gra Grogs!" getting closer. Little Dewi guided them across to the far side, where tall trees provided dark, welcoming shadows. Under the trees, a stream cascaded into the lake. This would be their key to finding Haydn. As the faint glow in the sky heralded a fine day the Grog boats could clearly be seen rounding the headland.

"Can they see us?" asked Essie anxiously, staring at the boats in horror.

"I doubt it," answered Little Dewi. "We're heading into this dark area. Look, they're separating! One lot is going straight on to the far side of the bay, to cut us off; the other is creeping around the shore, searching for us. They know we're in this bay somewhere and that we can't outrun them."

"There must be at least twenty of them in each boat," said Big Dewi, noting that the odds were not exactly in their favour.

The coracle glided under the trees. Big Dewi and Essie slipped over the side as quietly as they could – well, Big Dewi rather rolled out, like a sack of mouldy turnips. They swam ashore, whilst Little Dewi sank the coracle, to be recovered another day. Dawn streaks now warmed the sky.

The friends lost no time in following the merrily chattering course of the stream, running at first through thick woodland, until they had

to pause for breath. Would the Grogs realise they were following the stream, even though there was no path?

"This is the quickest way to Haydn's," gasped Little Dewi. "We have a bit of a start on the Grogs, so I think we must keep going along here."

"But they'll easily overtake us if we go at Big Dewi's speed," complained Essie. "He's like a snail with a Zimmer frame! If we leave the stream they are unlikely to find us."

Big Dewi snarled in her direction, "Yes, I know that, but we'll easily get lost then, and, anyway, they may not follow. Don't forget that their main purpose is to attack Aberdod."

Little Dewi was ready to continue and, as they set off again, he turned to Essie. "Look, Essie, if they catch us up, you must run like the wind. You're faster than any of us, so race on and get the message through, if we get involved in a fight."

On they went, stumbling in the semi-dark. Progress was slow. After pushing themselves to the limit, they again stopped, and drank from the stream. A sudden crack behind them caused them to whip round. A shadowy figure stood under the trees, in the half-light. The figure immediately emitted a high-pitched whistle-cum-yowl, sounding like half-man, and half-beast. Essie almost collapsed in fright. Big Dewi raced across towards it, but it melted into the

The two Dewis are avalanched off the cliff

undergrowth like an apparition.

"What was that?" stammered Essie.

"A Grog scout," answered Little Dewi. "That means they are after us and will be here fast. Let's get going."

The three Doddies ran on, finding the going easier in the improved light. From behind came regular whistle-yowls, indicating that the pursuers were getting closer. Big Dewi stopped.

"Go on," he said. "I'm going to silence the yowling."

He scrambled up into the branches of a bush. The others continued. It wasn't long before the Grog yowler appeared, stealthily moving across the rough ground with astonishing ease. As he passed under Dewi's bush, the big lad silently fell upon him, flattening the little Grog. Dewi hit him so hard that he wouldn't wake up for some time, then flung him into some bushes and ran off after his friends. They were waiting for him, not far ahead.

"He's been put to sleep for a while," announced Big Dewi. "There's not much doubt that they'll know by now, mind, that we're following the stream."

"Yes, but soon we cross it and head up the gorge," replied Little Dewi. "Hopefully, that will throw them, but we haven't a moment to lose."

The ground became steeper and soon they were out of the wood, with just the occasional tree to be seen. Although there was less cover, this was much pleasanter, as the sun now bathed them in warm, fresh, morning light. If only their quest had not been so hung with potential tragedy, this would have been a delightful hike. Their speed increased, but they kept throwing nervous glances over their shoulders. Eventually, they could make out a rugged slit in the cliffs on the opposite side of the stream: a craggy, shadowy gorge.

"Pant-y-goggin Gorge is that – the route up to the hermit's place," explained Little Dewi, who knew the area fairly well, for he had caught many frogs here. "We've got to cross the stream first, though."

Crossing such a fast-flowing stream was a major task for the little Doddies, even though they were brilliant swimmers. They continued upstream in search of an easier crossing.

"These logs will do," yelled Little Dewi, leaping on one and pushing out from the bank with the reed-stalk he had cut further down the valley.

The 'logs' were actually twigs, but large enough for Doddies. His companions followed and, for a few moments, they enjoyed the rush of the current as it carried them into midstream. Gradually, with their poles, the Doddies nudged their way over to the other side, laughing at the ease with which they crossed. Only Little Dewi spotted the human sitting on the bank, but he regarded most of these Grumpies, as Doddies called them, as being mainly harmless botchers, but best avoided because of their big, clumsy feet.

Sion Banc-y-felin sat on the sunny bank of the Nant-y-Goggin stream, watching the end of his fishing-rod. He rubbed his eyes. Having been doing a spot of night fishing, he now enjoyed the warm sunshine as he munched his last hunk of cheese. The stream gurgled musically as it tumbled down the wild *cwm*, and he fell into a stupor as he watched bubbles floating past. Then, he rubbed his eyes again. Was that a little figure he could see, floating past on a twig?

"Never," he thought, as the figure disappeared downstream. "Good grief, there's another one! It must be the Tylwyth Teg."

This time, he focussed on the figure – a little female, less than three inches tall, sitting on a twig and punting away with what looked like a dandelion stalk. Sion blinked and had started to rise, when he caught sight of a third figure sailing past. In his eagerness to investigate, his right leg slipped and he went up to his waist in a deep pool. Cursing, he gasped at the sudden cold, steadied himself, and then pulled himself out onto the grassy bank.

By then, the Doddies had swept past, out of sight. Sion gazed at the stream, expecting to see more of these strange little creatures, but apart from the butterflies and an occasional dragonfly, nothing stirred. His mind cast back to a couple of years ago, when he had caught sight briefly of a large frog hopping across a path, with a little figure on its back, down by the lake. When he had related the tale to his wife, Flopsy, she had dismissed him out of hand as being off his trolley. Since then, like many other Grumpies who came across a Doddie, he'd kept his secret to himself, afraid of being regarded as a stupid old fool.

Big Dewi grabbed an overhanging branch, managed to swing up onto the bank, and helped Essie out behind him. As he did so, he heard Little Dewi yell out. The current had caught him and towed the little lad downstream at a rapid pace. His reed-stalk had been torn from his grasp, and he clung on to the log for dear life, with a high waterfall approaching.

Big Dewi raced along the bank after his chum, with Essie close on his heels. He was not the fastest of runners, his rhythm more that of a Dutch barn trying to fly than an Olympic hurdler, for here he had to leap over all sorts of obstructions. Then, he caught sight of his friend. For the second time that day, Little Dewi was trapped on the spikes of a thistle – his log had caught in its stems just as he was about to be swept over the falls. Gingerly, Big Dewi reached out towards his mate, hanging on to

Essie's outstretched arm with one hand. Then, the inevitable happened. Essie lost her grip, sending Big Dewi hurtling into the river.

The big lad went in backwards, with a great splash. His immense posterior crashed into the water and instantly jammed between two rocks. With his head just emerging out of the fast-flowing stream, he sat in that ridiculous position, unable to move in any direction. Little Dewi saw his opportunity. Reaching out with his right leg, he stepped on to Big Dewi's head and, with a supreme effort, launched himself across the water and onto the grassy bank. This did not endear him to the big fellow, for the force of the move immediately caused him to submerge, take in great quantities of water and then rise back to the surface, his large nose gleaming like a Belisha beacon in the sunlight.

The action had loosened his anchorage, and he clung to one of the rocks, as Little Dewi offered him the end of a pole, which he grasped eagerly. Soon, they were lying on the bank, recovering their breath before making their way into the gorge.

"We seem to have thrown the Grogs off our trail," chirped Essie, sounding much happier now, "thanks to you, Dewi, stopping that scout. You were marvellous." She squeezed Big Dewi's hand, making him feel uncomfortable. He didn't like praise from Essie at all, and was much happier when she was rude

to him. That seemed more natural.

"They might still be after us," he grumbled, trying not to catch Essie's glance.

The going became fairly rough, as they struggled over boulder-strewn, uneven ground. Big Dewi constantly complained, as it was quite an effort to keep up with his more agile friends. Butterflies flitted across their path, caught in the strong morning sunshine.

"Isn't it strange," remarked Little Dewi, after a thoughtful silence, "how, even in the face of this appalling adversity, nature provides us with the strength and energy to overcome obstacles?"

"How d'you mean?" panted his big friend, stumbling along, and regularly glancing over his shoulder.

"Well, I'm enraged about the thought of Grogs destroying our village, and the way they're hounding us, and yet, I get tremendous strength from the beauty in these wild flowers, or even just the sparkle of the stream."

Big Dewi nodded. He struggled manfully to keep up with the others, aware that his friends back home depended on them getting a message through.

"I know what you mean, Dewi," said Essie. The lads found her lack of hostility rather odd. "We need the wilderness as much as the cultivated ground."

Shortly afterwards, they reached the head

wall of the gorge, a great rocky face that towered above them. Big Dewi sat down, his head in his big hands.

"We'll never get up that," he groaned, gazing at the crag in desperation. "We're trapped."

"Listen, you! We've got to get up it, for the sake of our friends," retorted Little Dewi, trying to hide his dismay. "I'll see if I can find a route up. Watch out for Grogs!"

Essie went off to look for other possibilities as he began climbing. He pressed himself against the sides and slowly made progress upwards, using pressure to keep himself up. Soon, he climbed out onto a wide ledge, about halfway up the face.

"Not as bad as it looks," he called encouragingly down to his reluctant companion, who still sat on a small boulder. "Tie this around your waist and I'll help you as you climb."

Little Dewi threw down the end of a cord, threading his end round a rock pinnacle. With no great enthusiasm, but well aware that Grogs might show up at any moment, Big Dewi tied himself to the cord, and walked towards the face.

"It's Mam Jones' cast-off clothes-line," explained Little Dewi, as he pulled up the slack to keep the rope taught whilst Big Dewi climbed. At first, things went well. To the accompaniment of a wide range of grunts, Big Dewi progressed up the cleft with the grace of a hippo. When he arrived at the narrowest part, unfortunately, his lower regions jammed in the cleft. He roared with anger, frightening Little Dewi, who quickly tied his end of the rope to the pinnacle, as he could sense Dewi was just about to 'go dull.' Big Dewi lashed out with his arms, hit the rock wall and shot out of the crack at speed, losing some height, until the rope held him – but only just. Mrs Jones' clothes-line was not meant for such tasks.

Big Dewi careered backwards across the face, until his enormous bottom crashed against a solid buttress. He then swung, like a pendulum, back across the rock wall, gathering speed. Little Dewi watched in horror as the big lad rocketed headfirst into a small sprig of heather that was growing out of the cliff. Big Dewi came to a sudden halt, his head jammed in its branches. With an almighty roar and a great thrust with his legs, he tore himself away from the cliff. Unfortunately, he brought the heather away with him, wrapped around his neck.

With earth, rocks, branches, leaves and debris crashing down, Big Dewi once more set off backwards, to pendulum across the cliff face, complete with his scarf of heather. This slowed him somewhat, and so, when again his bottom hit the far buttress, it was not quite so painful.

Back across the rock wall he went, getting redder in the face with each swing. When the heather hit the far cliff, Dewi thought his end had come: most of the branches and vegetation suddenly fell away, leaving him with a large branch festooning his hat. Slowly, the swinging eased, and he ended up dangling beside the cleft, looking up forlornly at Little Dewi.

Happily, his foot hung close to a small rock outcrop. He stepped on to it and pushed himself up a little. Little Dewi dropped down a loop of rope from the free end, so that his pal could slip his other foot through it and raise himself up to where his hands reached the ledge. Gaining his breath again, he managed to haul himself onto the ledge. Big Dewi was no climber.

Once again, Little Dewi led up the face, this time tackling the overhanging rock with skilful agility, taking advantage of every crevice and ledge to gain height. When he arrived at the overhang, despite his clumsy feet (Doddies were not designed with rock-climbing in mind), he managed to gain purchase on the shale crag. Then, as Big Dewi watched in horror, he swung out on his arms, his legs hanging freely in mid-air, before hauling himself up to safety in a series of three jerky movements.

"There's no way I'm going up there," yelled Big Dewi, and, getting no reply from his exhausted mate, he looked down the cliff and muttered dismally, "and there's no way I'm going down there." He would have great difficulty going up or down, and expected the Grogs to appear at any moment.

"I'll help to pull you up," shouted Little Dewi optimistically, as he threw down the end of the cord for his friend to tie on. He knew it would be hopeless, as he had nothing to which to anchor the cord – not even a blade of grass, but it was best not to tell the big lad. Big Dewi quickly gained the lower part of the overhang, moving at such speed that his friend could not possibly take in the cord quickly enough. At this point, perspiration blotted out all before Big Dewi's eyes; his violent breathing totally unbalanced him and, as he approached the overhang, he rocked about like a kipper hung out in a force ten storm. His head hit the rock with a resounding crash, and he saw only a blinding flash, before being dumped back down on to the shelf.

Dewi now had a raging headache, and it took some time before he once more regained his composure. Despite Little Dewi's pleading, he seemed set on staying put, not happy to climb up or down. With much cajoling from Little Dewi, he pulled himself to his feet and gazed despondently up at the overhang. Clearly, some incentive was needed.

"I've got a crumpet in my pocket," said

Little Dewi, knowing how much his friend enjoyed chewing Llandod crumpets.

This made Big Dewi's eyes twinkle. He thought of nothing but that crumpet. He got to his feet, checked the clothes-line and, then, steadily moved up towards the overhang. All went well, until his left leg caught in the cord and he fell violently against the bottom of the crag, striking it a considerable blow with his head. Again, Big Dewi saw stars – his teeth rattled and he scraped his left cheek against the rough rock, drawing blood, at the same time, hitting his left eye on a rocky spike. His eye instantly swelled and blackened, and quickly turned a deep purple with green streaks beneath the lower lid. His nose, an enormous honk that rivalled a rugby-ball, had taken a severe blow, and now, rather ignominiously decorated with a large slice of wet green moss, it took on a violent orange tinge, blackening rapidly at the edges. At this point, as he slid down the rock face, he resembled a lop-sided Guy Fawkes that had been on fire for several minutes: a most terrifying spectacle.

An ear-splitting roar like thunder rent the air as he began his fall. The whole overhang seemed to explode into bits, crashing down the cliff with Dewi. Bits of rock and boulders spewed in all directions, the avalanche hurtling past him as he fell back onto the ledge, oblivious to everything except his aching head, bleeding nose, black eyes, swollen cheek, scratched lips and bruised ears. Little Dewi, as the overhang exploded, descended rather quickly on top of the deluge, went flying over the ledge and passed his companion at speed. Luckily, as he reached the limit of the cord, Mam Jones' clothes-line gamely held, and the little chap hung above the drop, anchored to the bulk of Big Dewi.

After several minutes, Big Dewi recovered sufficiently to work out that things had changed somewhat. He looked around for his friend, and only when Little Dewi's calls for help reached him from below did he realise the poor lad's predicament. It did not take him long to haul the little chap up, as he was extremely light. Together, they sat gazing at each other's battered state, and wondering how on earth they could get out of this predicament. Time was passing, and the Grog fleet would be well on its way to Aberdod by now.

"Wow!" yelled Little Dewi, as he looked up at the devastated cliff. "There's tidy! The overhang's gone. You've knocked it down with that great forehead of yours. It should be much easier to get up now."

He was right. The climb to the top of the head-wall was now little more than a steep walk, much of it over the debris of rocks. After a few minutes of scrambling over unstable rocks, the two emerged at the top of the cliff,

At Haydn's door, Blaengoggin

and dropped thankfully on the grass, to lick their wounds. Big Dewi looked rather the worse for wear: his nose had swollen to twice its normal size and his face was a kaleidoscope of colours. One ear stuck out even more than usual.

"Where have you two been, all this time?" The question drifted across from the shade of a bush, where Essie lay on the grass, looking quizzically at the two lads.

"How did you get up here?" asked Little Dewi, sounding slightly annoyed that this female Doddie looked so laid-back and refreshed.

"Up the steps on the other side of the buttress to the left of the cliff," she explained, in an annoyingly self-gratified tone. "It was a delightful walk. What took you so long? You look dreadful, Dewi! Fighting, is it? Any sign of the Grogs?"

The lads ignored her questions. "Know-all," muttered Big Dewi under his breath.

"You should have seen what Dewi did to the cliff with that napper of his," said Little Dewi.

"Come on, we haven't a moment to lose." Essie stood up. "Let's get going. Old Haydn must be close."

"What about my crumpet?" yelled Big Dewi. He had suddenly remembered the offer as he chased after his friend.

They scurried through high grass, which, of course, slows down Doddies considerably. Old Haydn lived by himself in a disused rabbit-warren beneath a gnarled old oak, which made it easy to locate, especially once they came upon a well-used rabbit-run. This led them directly to Haydn's front door, which was set well back into the rabbit-hole, so as not to alert Grumpies to his presence.

"I hope this is the right hole," said Big Dewi as they groped in the semi-dark for Haydn's door-knocker. "Ah yes, here's the name – Blaengoggin. I can smell cooking. He must be having a late breakfast."

"He doesn't exactly welcome guests," remarked Essie. "Has he really got a killer budgie?" She pointed at the warning sign outside the door.

Their loud knocks summoned the occupant, who grumpily flung the door open and stood gazing at the three Doddies in complete disbelief. In their torn, wet rags, with their battered countenances, dishevelled hair and Big Dewi's remarkable colouring, they appeared like refugees from some pillaging campaign. Haydn the Hermit, thinking they were probably an advance party of the notorious Vandals of Llanfihangel Rhydithon, was about to slam the door shut, cursing the state of the nation, when Little Dewi choked out a greeting.

"Haydn, it's me, D D D-Dewi Bach," he stuttered.

Old Haydn did a double take, screwed up his face and shook his head in disbelief, gradually realising who these miscreants were. His uncombed hair gave him a wild appearance, which, together with his enormous beard and bushy eyebrows that hung over his eyes, revealed little of his face. His long apron brushed the floor, constantly re-arranging the dunes of dust that lay across the hearth. The whole place was a higgledy-piggledy mess, but the Doddies felt quite at ease here.

"Come in," he said enthusiastically, in the tone of voice that implies a certain understanding of eccentrics. Being one himself certainly helped him come to terms with this unusual visitation. "You'll be wanting a cup of tea, so sit down at the table, my friends, and tell me your troubles – you obviously can't be going around looking like that without having a great many problems."

The friends sat down, grateful for Haydn's understanding. He was a funny old stick but had a good heart. At one time, he had been snurting instructor at St Loosenuts School for Girls, but one pupil in his charge went under-water with an over-inflated snurting bag, which is rather like a bagpipe. When she released the faffing-valve, to begin playing, the bag propelled her through the water at incredible speed, and she was never seen again. Despite winning the Golden Snurt Trophy three times, Haydn retired after the accident. He increasingly became disillusioned with society in general and politicians in particular, until, eventually, he gave up everything and went to live as a recluse in a rabbit-warren. He still does a little snurting in private.

The Doddies related their story, or rather, Little Dewi gave the account, with frequent interruptions from his larger friend.

"We did hope you would lend us your frog to get one of us to Aberdod quickly," Little Dewi said hopefully, as he looked at the old hermit.

"I'm afraid old Fred hardly goes anywhere these days. Hopping into Aberdod is totally beyond him; he has gout in one of his rear legs and had another leg viciously bitten by a ginger Tom a few weeks ago," replied the hermit disconsolately.

The Doddies' hearts sank – now, there was no way to get home in time to save their friends.

3. The Battle on the Lake

THE WOODS ALONG THE SHORELINE resounded with yells and curses, as Grogs, with much thrashing about, fell over and ran into obstacles in the dark, in their search for the Doddies. Mayhem continued until some of the female Grogs appeared, carrying torches of burning embers from the fires, and they were able to see what they were doing. Hannie, looking rather battered, ran up to Ongut's tent as he arose from his bed.

"There's at least three Llandoddies in the woods. We caught one, but the others hit us and freed her. Then, they ran into the lake and made off in one of their little boats."

"Fools!" roared Ongut, grabbing Hannie by the neck and hurling her to the ground. As he moved to kick her, she rolled out of the way and scrambled out through the open doorway, with the Grog leader in pursuit, in a fiery temper. Hannie shot past Eingart, who turned to his leader.

"Master, let Hannie be and put some clothes on. It's not good for everyone to see you like that."

Ongut stopped, twitched, then raged defiantly for a moment, while his arms beat the air, and then, he retreated into his tent, realising how ridiculous he looked. On emerging, he ordered two fishing boats to chase the Doddies; he did not want his warriors diverted from the main attack on Aberdod. The boats set off at speed and were expected to catch the Doddies quickly.

Over breakfast, the masters of each war-boat sat in a council of war. Ongut left them in no doubt about their duty, as he stood aggressively in his black, armoured, combat vest bristling with spikes. Even when he offered you a biscuit, he gave the impression that he might tear your throat out. Since he had come to power, he had made enemies of all the Grogs' neighbours, and his men were constantly at war with the Un Shoor, a rather addle-minded tribe of hill-dwarfs, who dwelt in hills to the north-east.

"Forget the Doddies in the woods. They can't beat us to Aberdod in those stupid little craft that look like inverted beetles. The fishing crews can enjoy chasing them." Ongut paused, to slurp down a mouthful of toad-juice. "We'll sail shortly. Speed is vital if we are to reach Aberdod just after the Doddies have had afternoon tea. I've chosen today for the battle because it is St Cewydd's Day, when all Doddies celebrate. St Cewydd, the patron saint of rain, is dear to their hearts, so they will be even less likely to put up any resistance.

"No quarter must be given! All Doddie women must be taken, with all their cakes and cake-making equipment. This will ensure that we get a constant supply of cakes. Doddie men must be put to the sword, including all the old codgers; otherwise, they will try to counterattack. Young males can be brought back as slaves, or fed to the cats for our entertainment." As he broke off, the others cheered.

"What if they outnumber us, Ongut?" asked Gryphor, a short Grog with a pronounced limp, which he had acquired in a desperate fight with a stoat. It would be churlish to call him ugly – all Grogs are ugly.

"Aach! No problem. We should outnumber them two to one, and we all know that one Grog is worth three of them, so it is no contest," Ongut continued, with obvious contempt for Doddies. "There are more Doddies in the outlying areas, but they are too scattered to cause us a problem. We have better weapons. We can't lose."

The Grogs nodded in approval. Leila, who had returned to the camp after her battle with Big Dewi, came over and mockingly put her arm around Gryphor, with a broad smile across her face.

"Don't worry, Gryphor, I'll look after you."

As she patted the hilt of the sword hanging from her left hip, Gryphor shook himself free and angrily stormed off towards his boat.

"Where is Igrun?" asked Ongut, annoyed that the deputy leader still hadn't turned up.

"He's a little the worse for wear," replied Eingart, grinning broadly. "After getting drunk, he tried to sort out Leila, but she was ready for him. In his state, he was no match for anyone, let alone Leila. She hit him where it hurts and, while he staggered around, she beat him with something big and hard, so he's rather bruised this morning."

"That Leila will get what's coming to her, when I have a moment," said Ongut, twitching violently, and spilling his toad-juice over Eingart, as he deliberately avoided eye-contact with Leila.

The Grog warriors re-floated their war-boats. The boats were made of tanned rat-skin, light boats that could easily be transported across country. They were generally hauled ashore and secured with ropes, after a voyage. Whilst on water, they needed a certain amount of rock ballast to keep them upright. The vessels, with their high prows, their hawkish figure-heads

Saucy Sian under attack from Grog war-boats

and their overall black colour, looked sinister. Ballast was loaded, weapons stowed aboard, and the black Grog flag run up the single mast, as the warriors filed on board each vessel.

One by one, the boats pushed off from shore, the last warriors leaping aboard out of the shallow water. The long boom on each vessel slowly rose up the mast, trailing the huge black sail with its white Grog cake emblem in the centre. All Grog craft were named after cakes, their favourite food. Oars could also be used, but because the Grogs wished to retain their strength for the forthcoming battle they would rely on their sails to carry them to Aberdod. The fleet of war-boats glided out of the bay, followed by the support vessels carrying their camping supplies and food. Last to leave were the smaller fishing boats, which headed off in the opposite direction.

As they reached open water, the warriors began to chant to the rhythm of the beating of their shields with their fists, their voices low at first, then gradually rising to a high pitch. This war chant, designed to strike fear into the hearts of the enemy, reverberated across the water, terrifying to anyone who heard. The craft made fast progress before a fresh south-easterly breeze.

By mid-morning, with the sun high in a cloudless sky, the Grogs had settled down to a low hum, each boat taking a turn. In the lead sailed the Grog flagship, *Fondant Fancy*, with Ongut and two of his lieutenants on board. Where the war-boat prows rose to a high, hawk-like figurehead, a small platform provided an excellent viewing point for a look-out. Seydunk, the look-out on the *Fondant Fancy*, kept his eyes glued to the horizon. It would not do to miss anything whilst Ongut was on board.

Seydunk scanned the horizon ahead, trying to pierce the haze that hung over the water. Was that a speck he could see? No, nothing but water. There it was again, a slight, blurred spot in the haze. Again, it disappeared. Moments later, the speck reappeared, more prominent this time.

"Craft on the port bow!" yelled the look-out, alerting the signalman, who sat below him in the prow. As the boat swung to port to follow Seydunk's outstretched arm, various coloured flags were run up the mast, instructing all boats to follow the *Fondant Fancy*.

Ongut gave the order to beat the drum, signalling the war-chant, and quickly the chanting broke out, the warriors rhythmically beating their shields in an almighty din. Rapidly, they overhauled the distant speck. It grew larger and sharper as it emerged from the haze. Crews of the forward catapults swung into action. Grog catapults resembled cross-bows, and fired large, round rocks taken from the ballast channel. Without bothering to find out who he had in his sights, Ongut gave the order to fire. One after another, the missiles shot off in the direction of the strange craft, causing huge plumes of water with each splash. As so many fired at once, it soon grew difficult for each firing crew to assess which was their own splash, and hence adjust the aim for the next shot. The craft clearly turned to head away from the pursuing Grogs, and it soon became lost beyond the splashes.

After a huge barrage of splashes, Ongut gave the order to cease fire. When calm returned to the water, the Grogs gazed around in amazement. There was no sign of the other vessel. Surely, if they had scored a direct hit, there would still be some evidence of its wreckage, but they could see absolutely nothing. Ongut's brow knotted in puzzlement. The craft could not have vanished over the horizon – nothing could move that fast.

"Slow down, Kraa-col," he barked at the boat's skipper, and twitched nervously. "There's something odd about all this."

The fleet slowed to a crawl, every eye searching the water. With hardly a crest of a wave in sight, it would be impossible for any craft to hide. Ongut paced the deck uneasily.

"You saw that boat didn't you, Kraa-col?"

"Yes – yes, sir, I did, with my own eyes. It were there, as clear as a sprat on a spit!"

"We'll wait a few moments and then continue at speed" snorted the Grog leader.

The *Saucy Sian* bobbed about on the water, her four occupants lounging in the sunshine, drinking a Doddie brew, each sinking several delicious cakes made by Mam Llinos. The morning's fishing had not been too successful, but the break made up for the dismal catch: a minnow that had put up a terrific fight and almost pulled young Geraint over the side. Two days out of Aberdod, the four-man Doddie coracle, under the command of Captain Portly-Wobble, was intending to return home for the festivities of St Cewydd's Day, but their time estimations were somewhat wayward. Doddies never took anything too seriously, and so the lack of fish, or missing the festivities, did not worry the lads.

"We'd better get under way," said Dai Nant-y-Cwcw, a short chappie, even by Doddie standards. "Oh! What on earth is that lot over there?" His voice rose with urgency as he stared at the approaching vessels, black and menacing, that seemed to fill the horizon from end to end.

Captain Portly-Wobble jerked to attention and, with a practised eye, studied the distant boats through a telescope. Calmly and firmly, he gave his orders from the prow of the coracle.

"We'll move west at top speed, to get away from them, and hope that they'll pass by without spotting us. They are moving fast

Saucy Sian under water

and look very nasty … all in black, by the looks of it."

He broke off as all four thrust hard to build up speed. Because the crew sit looking to the rear they can observe the enemy easily when being chased. The black vessels gradually gained on them. Suddenly, as one, they all turned towards the Doddie craft, heading directly for them at speed. Geraint nearly fainted with fright, momentarily losing rhythm and slowing down the craft. All Doddies who operate coracles attend a course on synchronised waggling run by Martha Stiffjog. This is aimed at preventing the crew's legs kicking each other and losing rhythm.

"Waggle tidy-like, boys bach!" urged Captain Portly-Wobble. "They've seen us, alright, and they'll soon catch us up." He gasped for air, and then got his second wind. "They must be Grogs. I've never seen so many. That's their war-boats and they ain't here to garland us with flowers. Listen to that chanting – dreadful! – they don't have the harmony of Cor Aberdod."

"They're firing at us, the damn pirates" yelled Iestyn Coch, the fourth member of the crew, a startling sight with his shock of red hair, as the first missiles fell into the lake nearby.

The Doddies' legs thrashed harder than ever, but, in their panic to escape, the rhythm had gone. The Grog fleet was rapidly overhauling them. One huge rock descended from a high trajectory, crashed down just short of the stern of the coracle, and drenched the occupants with water.

"Oh, Mam fach," came the plaintive cry from Geraint, who was numb with fear. He'd never seen anything like this before. Each missile seemed to be directed straight at him, and he was so frightened that he could no longer contribute to the speed of the boat.

"Prrr-epare to submerge!" came the firm order from the captain, rolling his r's with determined emphasis. "Emerrr-gency dive Number 3, Standard Operating Prrr-ocedure, look you."

All Doddie sailors were well-drilled in emergency dives, the most effective way to escape from ducks and predators whilst on open water.

With missiles plunging down even closer, Captain Portly-Wobble directed his crew with well-oiled precision. He was aware that the enemy could no longer see his craft amidst all the plumes of water thrown up by the falling missiles.

"Keep your left leg in …
Take your right leg out …
Then shake it all about …
and into the deep we gallantly go!"

As one, the four Doddies extracted their right legs from the bottom holes in the coracle,

**Hauling Ongut
out of the water**

immediately rotated the legs clockwise, which caused the craft to keel over to port. Just before they all went under, the captain barked out, "Geraint, both legs out." Geraint, at the far end of the craft, withdrew his other leg. The coracle now moved forward slowly.

Portly-Wobble turned to the prow and raised the periscope through the top of the hawk-head. From just below the surface, he searched the surface of the water and could see the Grog boats now alarmingly close. They had stopped firing and seemed to be searching for the Doddie boat. He indicated the direction, and the coracle gently glided towards the Grog vessels. Doddies can stay under water for several minutes. They tried not to disturb the surface of the water, when they moved, so as not to betray their presence to the enemy.

The Grog fleet had stopped. The *Saucy Sian* ran under the nearest boat and Captain Portly-Wobble took out his large knife, determined to take some Grogs down with him. With great relish, he thrust the blade up through the skin of the war-boat, and hacked a great hole in the bottom. Little Dai immediately realised what his skipper was doing and he cut another great gash. The Grogs had no chance. The *Fondant Fancy*, for it was the flagship, rolled over on her beam ends and sank like a lead sausage, taking her crew down with her.

Sadly for the Doddies, they could not stay submerged for long and, one by one, they surfaced. Iestyn managed to take the coracle down to the lake bed, whilst Geraint, milling about amidst hordes of angry Grogs, found himself caught up in a net, as other war-boats closed in to rescue their comrades. He thrashed around, trying to break free, and then found himself dragged on to a boat. Captain Portly-Wobble tried to escape, but his round bulk was encouraged into a Grog net by means of a number of rather sharp spears, and soon he, too, ended up on a Grog craft, and trussed up like a turkey. Iestyn surfaced and followed the others into a net.

Dai Nant-y-Cwcw was made of sterner stuff. He surfaced, unseen, under the high stern of a war boat. Recovering his breath, he went under for a second time, to avoid the thrashing limbs of Grogs who were trying to get back on to their boats. As he went down, the crew of the *Fondant Fancy* re-surfaced, having freed themselves from their stricken craft. All Grogs are expert swimmers and easily escaped from the open boat. Ongut surfaced, roaring like a bull, his arms flailing about, and demanding to be rescued. Rapidly, the *Custard Slice* closed in and the crew hauled their leader out of the water, dripping like an old boot pulled out of a canal.

Ongut was not happy and began berating his warriors and demanding dry clothing. At this moment, Dai drifted under the *Custard Slice* and, with a gleeful grimace, sank his knife into her thin skin, quickly tearing a large hole in the bottom, and pulling himself to one side, to avoid being hit by the sinking boat. Ongut once again had that sinking feeling. He could not believe his eyes as the craft disappeared from under him, taking him and his comrades once more for a dousing in the lake.

Despite the rather precarious situation in which he found himself, Dai heaved with laughter, a common Doddie trait, even at the gravest of moments. He once again surfaced, almost splitting his sides with mirth, and immediately drew attention to himself. Moments later, he found himself caught in a Grog net and being dumped on the deck of a war-boat while still rocking with laughter. The Grogs were not best pleased. Anxiously, they looked for their leader. Ongut had been dragged right to the bottom of the lake by the sinking boat. He then shot up at incredible speed and reached the surface with a minor explosion of displaced water. This was followed by the usual display of roaring, until he was caught by a boat-hook and towed to the side of the *Brecon Tart*. The Grogs lifted him out of the water like an oily rag.

Leila

As Ongut changed into dry clothes, inside a large barrel on the deck of the *Brecon Tart*, the captain of the vessel tried to calm his agitated leader. The loss of two boats did nothing to improve the Grog leader's temper.

"I'll personally wring those Doddies necks," he said, coughing up lake-water and twitching alarmingly. At this point, he caught sight of Iestyn tied up and lying in a corner. "Aaarrgh!" roared Ongut, leaping out of the barrel in a fit of rage, and quite forgetting that he had no trousers on. He shot across the deck towards the astonished Iestyn, tripped over a coiled rope, shot over the side of the boat and landed back into the water. This involved yet another soaking and hauling back up, by which time, the Grog crew, weary of these antics, had stowed Iestyn away in another part of the vessel.

The fleet got under way once more, their sails filling as the Grogs headed for Aberdod. Whilst they had lost two war-boats, all their warriors had been recovered. All four Doddies found themselves tied up, unsure about their fate. The Grogs intended to use them to obtain local knowledge once they landed. Captain Portly-Wobble and Dai sat tied to a mast on the *Blueberry Muffin* and were left alone, but young Geraint had drawn the short straw: he was lying on the deck, tied to a low rail, on the same boat as the cruel Leila. She stood over him, hands on her hips, in a pose that made him cringe in fear. What did she intend to do with him? Thoughts raced through his mind, conjuring up all manner of horrors. Only a small lad, and bound up tightly, he felt utterly helpless. What could he say that would stop her harming him?

"I need something from you, scum," she snarled, her lip curling angrily as she moved her head from side to side. Her hand fondled the hilt of her sword, making Geraint squirm. He turned away and buried his head in an old sack that lay beside him, hoping she would go away.

Leila grinned and placed a boot on the wretched Doddie's stomach. With a sudden thrust, she rolled him over onto his back and stabbed her foot into his fat stomach. She held it there while he gasped in pain. She, then, whipped her sword out of the scabbard and raised it, as though she was about to chop his head off.

"P-Please! I'll tell you anything," Geraint gasped, by now rigid with fright. He thought of his Mam and sisters, and wondered what they would think of him ending up this way, trussed up like a turkey. This was worse than being chased by a duck. Leila laughed and swiped the air with her sword, showing how adept she could be with the weapon. It flashed down on poor Geraint and tore open the front of his smock from bottom to top, exposing a large amount of stomach. Again the sword flashed, this time severing his belt. Leila bent over the helpless Doddie, and, picking up a short length of stiff rope, she began to tickle his belly button. All Doddies are vulnerable to belly button-tickling. Geraint suddenly seemed to turn into a firecracker, jumping about all over the place, despite having been tied up. Leila paused.

"Who's the Doddie girl with pigtails and

freckles?" she asked in a low, threatening tone. "I have a score to settle with her."

"I don't know," gasped Geraint. He realised that she was talking about Essie, but could not, for the life of him, work out how she had upset this ferocious Grog.

"When I find her, I'll beat her up, and then take her eyes out and feed them to the crows."

Geraint quaked at the thought that he might also be up for the same treatment.

"Tell me about the Doddie defences," Leila continued. "How many warriors have you at Aberdod?"

The young Doddie tried to recover his breath, but Leila's knee was driving into the side of his stomach.

"We have no warriors," he gulped, "unless you count Mr Grime, the policeman. He's only got a little truncheon."

"You lie!" yelled the Grog, kicking the unfortunate Geraint viciously into a corner. Again her boot was on his stomach, and now she twisted it pitilessly, causing him to yell out in pain. At that moment, he blacked out and did not come round for some time.

Dewi Bach

4. Plas Llanmorg

THE SMELLS FROM THE KITCHEN at Blaengoggin were quite revolting, as the Doddies sat awaiting the breakfast that Haydn was cooking. After their supreme efforts, they all felt famished and in need of sustenance. Haydn had cleaned up Big Dewi's head with copious amounts of vinegar, so that, when he had finished, Dewi smelt like a stale chip-packet.

"What are we going to do now?" asked Essie in despair, her head in her hands. "No frog and no hope of reaching Aberdod in time to warn them."

"What on earth is he cooking?" Little Dewi mused, trying to go through the possible options, as his big friend sat snoring in Haydn's large, comfortable armchair, causing the table to rattle alarmingly at times. "Never mind, he's a good soul. Whilst politicians go around in their posh clothes and fancy accessories, Haydn speaks more sense and is totally incorruptible, even though he doesn't have two squrts to rub together!"

"Was it not because he was so fed up with politics that he came to live out here?" asked Essie, her eyes taking in the details of the rather jumbled living room.

"Yes, that's right. He hates greed and prefers the simple life, close to nature. All politicians seem to do is make things more difficult and costly for everyone. Haydn used to have endless arguments with the Potchers about some of the decisions they made for the so-called good of the Llandoddie community. He hated any thought of them introducing red tape, corruption or destruction of the environment, like Grumpie politicians are constantly doing. In the end, he felt so strongly about it, he left Aberdod to become a recluse. Ah! Here he is."

Haydn appeared, amidst a cloud of black smoke; he was carrying three large plates of badly charred offerings and humming a tuneless piece to himself. He could not be regarded as a culinary expert, by any stretch of the imagination. He plonked down the plates under the large noses of his guests.

"Dum, dum, dumity dum, – enjoy your meal," he said, settling down on a stool, still humming as though he were composing a lively concerto. "The kitchen is a wonderful place for generating ideas. I've just …"

"What's this?" asked Big Dewi, awakening from his snooze and gazing with disbelief at his breakfast.

"My own special veggie-breakfast," the hermit proclaimed proudly. "Pulverised beetroot with sprinklings of marsh-toadflax, fried in a crispy batter and then marinated in last Saturday's *consommé du grenouille*, and served with a sauce of eucalyptus sap-juice on a bed of desiccated rhubarb. Dum dum dum – no, that's not quite right for a snurting andante – much too fast." His mind was clearly fixed on a snurting melody.

The Doddies looked at each other, turning up their noses at Haydn's breakfast. Most Doddies are great fish-eaters, not fond of too much green stuff. Big Dewi looked sick and slurped his tea noisily.

"But, Haydn bach, it can't be a true veggie-breakfast if it contains *consommé du grenouille*," Essie protested. "Frog soup implies a certain amount of meat content."

"Couldn't I have a couple of fish-cakes, please?" pleaded Big Dewi.

"Indeed, you are right," Haydn replied, puffing thoughtfully at his enormous pipe and ignoring the big lad. "Strictly speaking, any …"

"Or, even just ONE fish-cake?" interrupted the desperate Doddie, trying to make himself heard by raising his voice several octaves.

"Some authorities, of course, regard six days as being a bit over-long in a maturing consommé." Essie was trying diplomatically to put across her concerns about the potential staleness of the breakfast, gesticulating in the air with her right arm, whilst at the same time, feeding the consommé into the plant-pot that stood nearby, and hoping the hermit did not observe the sleight of hand.

By this time, Big Dewi was beside himself, having anticipated a hearty meal, from the smells. He could take no more. He rose to his feet with a sudden jerk, strode across the room and, to everyone's amazement, hurled his breakfast, plate and all, out of the open window. "Blinkin' rubbish," he snorted rubbing his hands violently from side to side. "Not tidy enough even for a muck-spreader's donkey!"

Little Dewi and Essie were speechless at this total disregard for the hermit's kind, if eccentric hospitality. Haydn grinned amiably.

"I've got some biscuits in the cupboard," he said, and offered the biscuit tin to Big Dewi.

"It's OK, Haydn, I've got some Llandod fish-bangers in my pocket," said Essie, pulling out a few battered fish-bangers wrapped in leaves. "I can cook a quick breakfast of bangers and mash, while you come up with an idea for how we can warn the others." She disappeared

Grogs in pursuit

into the kitchen.

"As I was about to say, I have some of my best ideas in the kitchen." Once again, Haydn relaxed over his pipe, his bushy eyebrows twitching rhythmically. "The only chance you have to save your friends now is through Witch Coarsecackle. She has…"

"Witch Coarsecackle?" exclaimed both Dewis in unison, "No, no, anything but Witch Coarsecackle!"

"She's your only hope. I know it's a risk, but you must try. If anyone can get you to Aberdod in time, she can. You are still a long way from home."

They fell silent for a moment and looked at the old hermit. Doddies tried to keep well away from the witch and her erratic behaviour. She was seen sometimes around Aberdod, usually on her broomstick. When, on one occasion, she went into Mam Hackitt's café, the place emptied in seconds. Witch Coarsecackle, though generally well-tempered, was highly unpredictable, and could turn nasty at the drop of a hat. Policeman Grime had found to his cost that, when he issued her with a parking ticket for leaving her broomstick across his parking slot, she turned his trousers into a pink tutu and his helmet into a plant-pot containing a spray of miniature dandelions. When the unfortunate policeman tried to catch her, she turned his feet into large blocks of lead, which he suffered

for several days, until she took pity on him. She had a thoroughly mischievous streak and created a veritable hell for anyone who crossed her. But, many times, she had shown kindness, often when least expected. It all depended on the mood of the day.

"You're right, Haydn," agreed Little Dewi, after a while. "We have no option. Let's get going as quickly as possible."

"Oh dear," breathed Big Dewi, trembling for the third time that morning. He did not relish meeting that old witch in her lair. At that moment, Essie returned with three portions of fish-bangers and mash, which they all wolfed down eagerly. They had nearly finished their meal, when they heard a noise outside.

"There's someone out there," said Haydn, looking puzzled. "It's unusual for me to have any visitors at any time – why so many now?" He rose from his chair, walked over to the open window and poked his head out. Immediately, he turned and quietly shut the window, his face looking drawn.

"I'm afraid there are Grogs outside," he explained. "They seem to be searching the area. There are a lot of them and they look pretty nasty."

"They must have seen us from a distance, when we were climbing the head-wall," commented Little Dewi. "If they lost our scent down by the stream, that would explain their delay. This is a natural route from the top of the gorge, so they are probably wondering which way to go now. It's unlikely they are aware of this place, as it's set back into the hole."

"Agreed, unless they explore the hole, notice the window, smell our breakfast or see the plate Dewi threw out," said Essie sarcastically, once again feeling threatened. "Is there a back way out of here, Haydn?"

Haydn had gone into the kitchen, to put out the fire. He then bolted the front door, grabbed a large pole and addressed the others.

"They are unlikely to try to enter, but we must leave quickly by the back way. It means some distance of walking through the rabbit-warren, but it's fairly easy and I'll take a torch. Follow me."

The Doddies walked along the dark passage in single file, glad to be on the move again. After they had come some distance along the uneven tunnel, stumbling over leaves and twigs, they emerged past Haydn's wicker gate and out into the July sunshine.

No Grogs could be seen on this side of the bank. Haydn set a fast pace across the moor, with his wide-brimmed hat jammed down over his mass of wayward hair. The hat insulated him from people, helping him to feel secure, and kept others at a distance. At each step, he thrust his great pole forward, humming with determination. The distance to Plas Llanmorg,

the witch's house, was not far, but fraught with all manner of strange obstacles, as befits a witch, and there was no knowing what the Grogs might do. Haydn, perhaps, knew Witch Coarsecackle better than most, as they were almost neighbours, but he tried to hide his dread at the thought of meeting her. Each of them kept a strange silence, deep in their own thoughts and anxieties about what lay ahead.

Soon they came to a hill. The going became craggier and the views more extensive as they gained height. These hills were like mountains to the Doddies – even a mole-hill took some effort to climb. From their vantage-point, they looked around for any signs of pursuit. On the bare hill, they were highly conspicuous, and when they scanned the moors they had just crossed, they could see many dark figures in the distance, heading rapidly towards them.

"There they are!" cried Essie. "They've seen us. Come on, we can't delay a second."

She ran on. The others followed as best they could, with Haydn pointing out the way. They descended into a rocky gully and crossed a shallow brook that tumbled down the rocky bed. After quickly refreshing themselves at a waterfall, they followed a track that wound up under a great cliff. A narrow ledge slanted upwards across the face of the cliff, and the hermit led the Doddies along it. At this point,

Essie accidentally dropped a brightly-coloured scrunchie.

"This ledge is known as *Llwybr-y-wrach,* the witch's path. I've not been up here for a long, long time," Haydn said in a hushed voice, as though trying to prevent anyone overhearing their conversation. "Rock-falls sometimes carry away part of the cliff. Pray that she doesn't play any tricks on us."

The others knew who 'she' was, for the witch dwelt heavily on their minds.

"Do you think she knows we're here?"

"She does now."

A raven took off from a nearby crag, soared over them and flew out of sight round the cliff.

"That bird has been watching us for some time. I'll bet he's off to tell the old witch that we're on our way. I'm hoping that the Grogs don't know of this route and won't see us up here. Dum, dum, dumpty-dum." Haydn carried on, slowly gaining height, his melodious snurting tune getting louder.

"Why does he sound so happy?" Big Dewi was confused.

"I think he's trying to calm his nerves," suggested Essie.

The four friends scrambled over occasional awkward sections. As they climbed, the drop on their left became more frightening, for the ledge narrowed dramatically. The cliff scenery became grimmer, the rocks of black and red

Haydn vaulting over the snail

looking more and more threatening and sinister. Now, there was no birdsong, and dark clouds rolled across the sky as though heralding some disaster. Then, a snail came slithering down the ledge towards them. It looked enormous to the friends, and it completely blocked the ledge as it slowly lurched towards them.

"Follow me," yelled Haydn. He ran up the ledge towards the snail, and, amazing the Doddies with his agility, he pole-vaulted clean over it, deftly dodging the antennae. Little Dewi hesitated, weighing up the on-coming creature. He did not have a pole, but, with a sudden rush, he raced up to the snail and took a flying leap onto its shell. Momentarily he tottered, then, with one stride, crossed the shell and jumped down on the far side, into Haydn's arms. Essie, without hesitation, followed Little Dewi's example, only with more grace, and letting out a wild yell as she did so.

Big Dewi, less sure on his feet, did not relish the prospect of flying through the air above this lurching beast, with that awful drop to his left. The snail was now almost upon him, so he retreated back down the ledge. He was no athlete, and the short distance between the snail's antennae worried him: could he really leap through the gap? He marshalled every scrap of courage he possessed and took a long run at the snail. Dewi leapt forward, but his left foot caught the right-hand antennae as it retracted. With a crash, he hit the shell and fell back in front of the advancing snail.

Before he could get out of the way, the snail was upon him. Big Dewi, flat on his back, felt the slimy trail of the snail move across his body. Then came that most awful of moments, as anyone who has undergone the experience will recognise, when the snail grasps in a vice-like grip whatever it is moving over, and drags itself forward. Dewi found himself caught in the energy-sapping hold, each part of his body compressed as the snail dragged itself onwards, repeating the process as it continued. He underwent agonizing contortions, and, as the snail moved on, a trail of slime covered him. He pondered the words of Martha Stiffjog, who led adventurous activities with the Doddie Guides, and was something of an expert on snail-combat: 'If a snail gets on top of you, the best course of action is to bite one of its tubercles. It will quickly roll over.'

Dewi could not bring himself to sink his teeth into the beast. He tried to protect his face but his head became jammed in an all-embracing, suffocating grasp, completely disorienting him. Suddenly, his head popped out of the grip, his face coated with revolting slime, and he all but passed out. He tried to move, but the snail was too heavy. It took

Opposite: Plas Llanmorg

some moments for the beast to climb over and continue its slimy way down the ledge, much to Dewi's relief. The others helped to pick him up, as he wiped his face with the front of his smock.

"Uugh! That was dreadful!"

He had no sympathy from the others, who were splitting their sides with laughter. Their laughter quickly evaporated, when a party of Grogs appeared on the other side of the snail. Essie took off up the ledge as fast as she dared, followed by Haydn and Little Dewi. Big Dewi paused to watch the Grogs briefly, and then continued at a steady pace, sure that it would take their pursuers some time to pass the snail. They were all anxious to be off this frightening ledge, especially now that the Grogs were following. Below them, cliffs, vegetation and rocks fell away into unfathomable depths, and the path had been greatly eroded in places. It was a terrifying experience. Higher up, Essie looked back and had a long range view of the Grogs, who were dealing with the snail.

Without any remorse, the Grogs began hitting the snail with their clubs. As its head and antennae retreated into its shell, several of them grasped the bottom of its shell and started to rock the creature back and forth. Essie watched in horror. They gave an almighty heave and sent the snail hurtling over the edge of the precipice. On they came, about two dozen of

them, moving rapidly up the ledge after the ambling Big Dewi. Essie wondered what to do if they came to a dead end. The prospect was terrifying. She shouted at Big Dewi to get a move on. Shortly, they came to where a large section of the ledge had been cut away, and poles had been placed across, to bridge the gap. As Haydn made to step onto the 'pole bridge', it slid away to the far side.

"It's Coarsecackle's magic," Haydn snorted in indignation, as the bridge disappeared. "We can't jump that distance." The others looked for another route.

"There's no alternative here," Haydn anticipated their thoughts. He turned back and joined them. At that moment, the bridge slid back across to cover the gap.

"Blasted thing," growled Big Dewi in disgust. Suddenly, he charged forward at speed, trying to reach the bridge before it could disappear. Perhaps it was fortunate, but, as he shot forward, he tripped over a low rock, crashed onto the ledge and was grabbed by Haydn, before he fell over the edge.

"Gee! Did you see that?" yelled Little Dewi. "That bridge moved with the speed of a Phyrgian Thunderbolt. You didn't stand a chance, Dewi, so don't try any more dull capers."

Not for the first time, they thought that this must be the end of their quest. There seemed to be no way past this ridiculous bridge. Essie weighed up the situation thoughtfully.

"We need to tackle this intelligently. If you three stay there and keep waving your fists at the bridge, and moving about without getting any closer, I'll try a sneak approach," she said, and then bent down on her knees and slowly lowered herself over the edge of the cliff.

"Essie fach, that's dangerous," yelled Big Dewi in horror, half thinking he should pull her back up.

"I'm OK. You just get back there and watch out for the Grogs. They'll be here any moment."

She hung by her arms from the ledge, which, luckily, had a series of firm ridges that she could cling to as she made her way hand-over-hand towards the bridge. Whilst this was happening, Big Dewi collected as many stones as he could find, ready to deal with the Grogs.

"I see what she's doing," muttered Little Dewi. "If we engage the bridge's attention, it might not notice her sneaking up on it from below. Keep distracting the bridge, Haydn."

To any casual observer, the sight of Haydn and Little Dewi making rude gestures at the bridge, and yelling obscenities at it would have given grave cause for concern about their sanity. Slowly, Essie edged closer. The bridge stayed put. With a final lunge, she grabbed it with her left hand, before it could pull away. Essie swung across the gap as the bridge carried her across to the far side. There, she could easily climb up on to the continuation of the ledge-path.

"Brilliant work, Essie," yelled Haydn, applauding the girl's astonishing effort. "Throw her the cord, Dewi."

The cord was thrown across and Essie tied it to a rocky spike. When both sides were secured, Haydn came humming his way across the gap, having threaded the cord through his enormous belt, to afford more security. At this moment, the first Grogs appeared round the bend and, seeing the friends, they ran forward at a charge.

Big Dewi was waiting for them. With a fusillade of stones he stopped them in their tracks. Two Grogs were badly hurt. They changed tactics. Two or three of them had shields, and they put these together and moved forward slowly. Dewi's stones bounced off the shields, apart from occasionally hitting an arm or leg. Steadily they advanced. Haydn was safely across, and it was Little Dewi's turn. He moved as fast as he could, but absolute care was needed on the traverse.

Big Dewi wondered whether to charge the Grogs and knock as many over the edge as he could, but he realised it would only be a matter of moments before he would end up sharing the same fate. Although not warriors, these fisher-Grogs were no push-over. Running short of stones, he grasped a rotten piece of wood, covered in lichens and grass, and whirled it round his head, ready to throw at the Grogs. Pollen inside the vegetation must have set him off, for he suddenly gave a resounding sneeze, so loud that it echoed across the far side of the valley. The Grogs stopped in astonishment at the sound, which had caused some vibration on the cliff. A small rock moved, then another. Suddenly, above them, the cliff gave way and a massive avalanche of rock and earth crashed down, sweeping all the Grogs over the edge. Dewi could hardly believe it. Did his sneeze really do that? At least, now there was no immediate threat from the Grogs.

It was his turn to cross the gap and he went over without delay. Would the much-battered cord hold him? He inched his way across, with the cord stretching almost to breaking-point. He progressed slowly and, thankfully, reached the far side without mishap, and sat down for a few minutes, to recover.

The four intrepid friends continued cautiously up the ledge, each wondering what might happen next. Soon, they turned round a corner in the cliff and the ledge broadened out into a wide path. Just past a large crag on the edge of the precipice, they looked up in awe. High above them rose Plas Llanmorg, a tall, gaunt, grim, grey, fortified house with several towers. The building was linked to the main cliffs by a slender bridge, *Pont-yr-ellyll*. As they gazed fearfully at it, the sky darkened. The sun disappeared, blotted out by black clouds. Day became night. The wind freshened and, with an ear-shattering crash, a tremendous clap of thunder rent the air. Thunderbolts flashed across the sky, out of orange, fiery clouds, and it began to rain like a monsoon.

To the deafening crashes of thunder, the Doddies ran across *Pont-yr-ellyll,* trying not to look down at the horrifying drop on either side of the narrow bridge. Beneath them, dramatically illuminated by intense lightning, the Impalers rose out of the misty depths of the gorge. These huge fangs of rock could rip a body to pieces, should anyone be unlucky enough to fall. As Big Dewi ran ponderously after the others, he had just cleared the bridge when it exploded into a million crystals, lighting up the cliffs with an infinite variety of colours. In absolute horror, the friends gazed back at the gap left by the bridge. There was no escape now. They gingerly climbed the final steps that curved up to the forbidding house and stopped in the dark porch, beneath two fearsome stone gargoyles. At each flash of lightning, they sought a bell-pull. Eventually, Big Dewi found it by feeling around the door. He gave it a terrific wrench and a hollow clanging resounded from inside. They stood in a huddle, not sure what would happen next.

Nothing.

"Try it again," whispered Haydn. Big Dewi yanked the bell-pull and the hollow noise boomed out once more. As the clanging faded away, still nothing happened.

"We'd better see if the door opens," said Little Dewi, timidly, from behind the others.

Big Dewi grasped the huge door-knob, twisted it and pushed the massive oak door inwards. With an agonisingly loud creak, the door slowly swung open. Hesitantly, they stepped into the dark interior. Creeping into the great hall, the four friends gazed around in the dim light. Suddenly, with great force, the huge door through which they had entered slammed shut with a crash, cutting them off from the outside world. A chill ran through their spines, for it seemed like the door of a prison closing on them. The warmth of the July morning had gone; inside this dungeon-like hall, they felt the chill of an evil presence somewhere deep inside.

Grog Warrior

5. The Portrait

"OH, NO!" GULPED ESSIE, wide-eyed at the sight of this dark hallway, with its atmosphere of impending menace and unknown horrors. She clung tightly to Little Dewi as they tried to make out shapes lurking in the dimness.

"At any moment, something nasty is going to appear," thought Little Dewi, trying to overcome his unbridled imagination, not daring to voice his concerns, in case the others took fright. His immediate desire was to get back out through the door as fast as his legs would let him, but his feet seemed to be glued to the large stone slab on which he stood. He felt completely drained of strength, unable to do even the simplest thing.

Their eyes slowly became accustomed to the dim light. They stood in a huge hall, surrounded by walls of dark stone, from which, spaced at intervals, there protruded flaming torches on metal brackets. Spiders' webs dripped from the brackets, silvered in places by the light. Doors led off two of the walls. A wide, open staircase ran up the right-hand wall, which was decorated with the fierce heads of savage creatures. A snake, a water-fiend, a horned monster and other diabolical shapes rose into the Stygian blackness at the top of the stairs. The intruders tried hard to avoid gazing at them.

Something brushed against Little Dewi's right ear. He almost jumped out of his skin in fright, and turned to see the dim outline of a shaggy, wild head above him, its long hair just touching his head. Did it move on its iron bracket, or…?

"Yes, it's moving!" screamed Dewi, his thoughts breaking out into a choking voice, panic-struck in desperation.

The grotesque head lurched, and then crashed down on top of Little Dewi, knocking him to the floor. Essie watched in horror, and when she saw the head come down, she fainted and slumped down beside Dewi.

"There's something up there."

Haydn defiantly rained blows with his pole on the iron bracket above, and some sort of creature scurried into the dark recesses of the upper wall.

"It's OK, Dewi," comforted the hermit,

bending down to help the little chap to stand up. "I think a spider must have dislodged the head from its bracket."

Dewi was not convinced and sat muttering incoherently on the floor for several minutes. Big Dewi tried to revive Essie, but it took some time. He hadn't seen the head fall, but when the other two had fallen down, it took his mind off the horrors of his imagination. After a few minutes, both were on their feet again, but still shaken.

"Do we go up the stairs, or into one of the other rooms, is it?" asked Little Dewi, gesturing towards the rooms.

"I'm going out … fast," came Big Dewi's voice from the rear. He moved a pace back and turned the door handle, which instantly fizzed into a blinding blue flash, turned gold, and then sent a shock through the Doddie's arm that knocked him back across the floor with such force that he hit the far wall.

"I don't think we're meant to leave at the moment," interjected Haydn. "Why don't we try … ?"

"Aaaaaaaach…aha ha ha ha ha ha ehe ehe ehe he he!" A wild, hysterical cackle resounded from the upper reaches of the house, causing the friends to freeze in abject fear. The witch was obviously at home. The inane cackling continued for a few moments, and then it degenerated into a coarse, low-toned,

throaty croak. This was followed by a violent swish-swash sound, as though something nasty was flying through the air, and it ended with a terrifying crash. This was followed by lower, unidentifiable noises.

"We'd better go up the stairs and confront the old witch as quickly as possible," said the hermit, putting down his stick and starting slowly up the stairway. This was the last thing the others wanted to do, but they followed reluctantly and at a distance, ready to run if things got too hot, though that would hardly have saved them. Keeping their eyes on the darkness ahead, and half-expecting demons to emerge at any moment, they crept upwards, shaking with fear. Once on the first floor, they realised that the sounds were coming from still higher up. As they climbed higher, a faint light attracted their attention. All eyes focussed on an open door, leading off the landing above, from which the light grew brighter. A floorboard creaked ominously. Little Dewi jumped out of his skin, when something cold and wet wriggled up against his cheek in the dark. He leapt back and lashed out with one hand, but hit only thin air. Was that a hand-rail he could make out beside him, or was it a snake about to strike? They stood beside the open door, trying to see inside, but a Welsh dresser blocked the view. Essie clung tightly to Big Dewi's arm, but so frightened was the lad that he didn't notice.

"Aaaaaaaggghh aha ha ha ha ha ha ha ha." The cackling tailed off into a coarse gurgle, from inside the room. "Come in, my little darlings."

The absurd, high-pitched voice was strangely compelling, hinting that the witch had been aware of their every move. Haydn cautiously led them into the light, quaking, even though he had met Witch Coarsecackle on several occasions. This was the first time he'd been inside her house.

In what seemed like part play-room, part laboratory and part library, a jumble of strange objects lay strewn around in complete disorder. True, most of the books stood on bookshelves, but many lay all over the room, with one large book propping up a table. In one corner stood a covered bird-cage, in another was a cobwebby skeleton. The main table was festooned in weird charts that were spattered with coloured symbols, blackened shapes of savage beasts, and objects that the Doddies had never seen before and never wanted to see again. Scattered across the floor was a variety of objects, most of which the Doddies would have described as rubbish, whilst underneath some papers, a large orb glowed with a strange green light.

In the centre of the room stood a deformed little chap with an enormous head and the ugliest face that Big Dewi had ever seen. Next to him rose the tall figure of Witch Coarsecackle herself, clad in a bright green robe decorated with mysterious symbols, and a small pointed hat on top of her long, green and yellow hair. In her right hand she held a long, red stick with a gungy green blob on the end of it. As the four entered, she looked across and gazed at them with a glare so fiery that Little Dewi thought it would burn right through him. Big Dewi took off his cap and wrung it in his hands – this was the first time he'd taken it off in three years, which showed how worried he must have been.

"Ah! Haydn, I see you've brought me some little playmates!" Her voice had become surprisingly sultry, almost playful. The Doddies remembered her penchant for mischief. "What shall we do with them, Snizu?" she directed her question at her strange servant, who stood expressionless.

"You could …" Hardly had Snizu uttered the words than the witch exploded, crashing a bottle of *Crème de Menthe* down on his ugly head. Essie, until this point, had been petrified with fear. She sprang behind the bulk of Big Dewi and crouched, biting her nails and trying to make herself as small as possible.

"Shut up, you pooh-faced little worm," screamed the witch, with such force that the Doddies leapt back a step. "Stand still! I'm supposed to be painting you."

She lifted the red stick and poked Snizu in

The four friends
at the bottom of
the stairs in Plas
Llanmorg

Coarsecackle painting Snizu in robust style

the left eye with it, turning his eye into a messy green shape. Little Dewi realised that the stick was actually a badly worn brush; he gasped as she picked up a massive heap of yellowy-brown paint from a rather filthy palette, only to stuff it into Snizu's right ear and drag it down across his cheek, to end with a terrific swipe of neat paint that she deposited on to the tip of his nose. Haydn gazed in admiration at this, for although it showed a cruel streak, in more senses than one, he clearly saw artistic prowess in the bravura display of brushwork.

"So, why do you enter my house unannounced?" the witch demanded, as she picked up a wide brush and dipped it into a heap of foul-coloured paint. Her voice had now become extremely deep, gravelly and threatening, as she seemed to take on the role of another character. Behind her, on an easel with a ferocious-looking bird on top, stood a large, untouched canvas. Even the easel looked menacing. The Doddies wondered why she was painting on Snizu's face and not the canvas.

"Ma'am," stuttered the old hermit, trying to elongate the word as long as possible, in the most cringing manner he could summon, "we tried the doorbell, but received no answer …"

"Three times," interjected Big Dewi, instantly regretting that he'd said anything, as he stood tugging his beard nervously.

"Aachh… sscccchhnnorrrr …" The witch gave the most dreadful snort, at the same time flinging her brushes into the air. They fell to the floor, turned into chickens, that shot off under the furniture, squawking. It reminded Dewi of his sadistic maths teacher, a most terrifying prospect. "You lie! You only rang twice."

Her hand shot out and pointed towards Big Dewi's feet. His boots glowed bright crimson, then ignited like rockets and thrust the poor fellow upwards at speed. He hit the chandelier overhead at a cracking pace, jammed there, and, at that moment, the chandelier began to revolve at phenomenal speed. Big Dewi was simply a blur. Essie determined that she would not say a single word until she got out of this madhouse.

"Aaaha aha aha ha ha ha ha." The witch cackled alarmingly, and then, as the room began to shake with Big Dewi's revolutions, she decided it was time to end the game. She waved her hand, the chandelier came to a sudden stop and Big Dewi catapulted out of it like a cork from a champagne bottle. He crashed into a bottle of *Chateau de Plonquers,* spilling its contents over himself. He lay on the floor for several minutes, in a dazed heap, becoming quite blotto on the deliciously intense red wine. Essie knelt down to comfort him.

"So, why have you come?" This was little short of a scream, as she plastered Snizu's face with a painting knife. Thick purple paint hung from his large nose.

"Beggin' your pardon, Ma'am, but we're in trouble," volunteered Little Dewi.

"Aaaagh, you've come to the right place for TROUBLE!" Coarsecackle gleefully stuffed a large wedge of thick Ultramarine paint up Snizu's left nostril, giggling shrilly at the absurd effect she had created. "I do love portrait painting." Her voice changed from delight to anger in an instant. "… but I only have this cretinous, ugly, sheep's backside of a face to paint. I need a new model." She turned round and looked sternly at Little Dewi. "Do you pose, little Doddie? Probably not, with a honk like that, but at least you would make a change from this slime-sucker!" Her voice rose again as she clouted the poor Snizu across the left ear, this time with a bottle of *Concha Toro Sauvignon Blanc,* with its rich tropical fruit aroma and hint of apples. Snizu flinched, the witch waved her hand, and the broken bottle turned into a box of chocolates. Whilst her attention was diverted, Little Dewi had crawled hastily behind a large settee. He was not too keen on being painted in the rather robust manner of Snizu.

"He he he," giggled Big Dewi, as he sat in a pool of wine. His nervousness had evaporated. The wine was taking effect on him. Perhaps, he found the thought of Coarsecackle painting his friend rather amusing.

"The Doddies are about to be invaded and we need to warn them quickly," said Haydn, trying to keep the witch off Little Dewi's back, and push along their quest before it degenerated into disaster. "Can you help us get …?"

"Phthurp!" Big Dewi stuck out his tongue, made a dreadfully rude noise and went into uncontrollable giggling.

The witch, lurching from mild mischief to downright sadism, seemed to grin as she flashed her hand in the direction of the settee, once again giggling gleefully. A blinding flash stopped Haydn's words, and Little Dewi's trousers turned into a trapeze and hung itself from the ceiling, beside the bird-cage. It had somehow fastened itself to Dewi's ankles, and now it hauled him into the air, to hang upside down. At this point, a feathery head appeared from under the cover of the bird-cage. Attached to it was an extremely long beak, which proceeded to peck Little Dewi's bottom, precisely on every half-minute, producing a pained yelp each time. This caused Big Dewi to roll over on the floor and laugh hysterically.

"I haven't time for your silly games," declared the witch, obviously relishing her own silly games, as she flicked daubs of paint across Snizu's face. "We've nearly finished, Snizu."

The servant was well aware that to express pleasure that his ordeal was almost over would land him in further trouble, so he stood motionless, gamely taking all that was hurled at him. A large dollop of cadmium orange landed on his much-abused nose.

"But the Grogs will massacre all the Doddies and… " Haydn by now was getting desperate.

"Grogs! Grogs, did you say?" screamed Coarsecackle, her voice again rising to a shrill, almost unintelligible yell. "Where are the Grogs?"

Haydn realised he now had her full attention, as, for some reason, she clearly hated Grogs.

"They are crossing the lake in a fleet of war-boats, and planning to attack the Doddies after tea. These three overheard their plan and came to me for help. They need to get to Aberdod as quickly as possible."

The witch scowled thoughtfully and, when Snizu looked quizzically at her, she smashed a superbly mellowed bottle of *Vin du Roussillon* on his now wet head. He tried hard to appear not to have noticed Coarsecackle's lively manner of expression, and barely flinched.

"The painting is done," she snorted, pointing both hands at the canvas. Immediately, the canvas began to crackle, and sparks flew off as various colours swirled round on its surface. An image emerged gradually from the swirling mess: the exact portrait of Snizu that she had just painted on his face, each brush-stroke faithfully rendered, betraying a profoundly penetrating portrayal of a

Little Dewi on the trapeze

pillock. With a final flourish of her brush, she embellished the background of the portrait by suggesting a distinguished castle interior, dimly-lit in the manner of Rembrandt, though Snizu's strangely-adorned features implied a definite superficiality of drama. Haydn gasped, impressed at such a masterful display.

"Tomorrow, I shall enjoy using the portrait

for target practice. You are dismissed, you beetroot-faced, shrivelled-up little toad – no, you're not. As a reward, make us some *cawl*. At once!" Snizu shot off like lightning. At the same time, Little Dewi fell back down to the floor and picked himself up, a little sore and very red.

The Doddies and Haydn watched the witch with bated breath, wondering what might happen next. She crossed to the window, stuck her head out, holding her long, thin nose tightly, and blew a thunderous, rippling, rasping noise that sounded like a defective Alpenhorn. Before she had time to utter a word, a small bird arrived at the window. She spoke to it in some strange guttural language, and it flew off at once.

"Come, we will go down for some *cawl*. It's one of my hotchpotch soup recipes, with bat's-brain dumplings and toad-bladder croutons."

Her manner had changed. She led them down the stairs, to another chaotic room, with the others supporting Big Dewi, who was walking unsteadily, in his tiddly state. Could this be the kitchen – or perhaps the stables? It was certainly in a mess. Snizu had prepared a pot of slurge-green, bubbling liquid, which Coarsecackle described as *cawl*, but the Doddies were not convinced. They pretended to sip the liquid, trying especially to avoid the toad-bladder croutons, as they all sat around the table. When Little Dewi thought the witch

wasn't looking, he tried the trick of emptying some of the stomach-churning *cawl* into a flower-pot. The flower immediately exploded and turned into a grotesque skull on a stalk, smouldering for some time afterwards. The huge pile of cakes in the centre of the table looked inviting, but the Doddies were rather taken aback when the pieces of *Bara Brith* loaf got up and made their own way across the table to each person's plate.

They discussed the situation with the witch, who emphasised her hatred for Grogs. She related how, when she was a little girl, one day, a band of Grogs broke into the house. Only her *tad-cu,* or granddad, was in the house at the time, and, unfortunately, old *tad-cu* was so deranged that his feeble spells simply produced chaos. The Grogs beat him up, created mayhem, and ran off with many valuables. So, the witch was keen to take her revenge at every opportunity. She promised the Doddies a raven to fly them home, although she had some trouble convincing them that the raven would be tame enough to respond to their instructions. Even Essie began to warm to her, but still kept her mouth firmly shut.

"I wonder if it would be worth one of you going to Colonel Gnowse-Pickering, to see if he can help you out with his frog cavalry squadron," commented Haydn. "The colonel can be a little awkward at times, but if you emphasise how he may lose the privilege of occasional Doddie cakes, he may see reason."

The squadron was part of the Elfael Field Force and often assisted Llandoddies at times of strife, for the Doddies themselves did not possess an army. The EFF belonged to the Twerpanis, little hill folk, who lived to the east of Llandod. They occasionally rescued the Doddies from raids by the Howey Trolls.

"I have two ravens available, and so two of you will have to ride together," declared the witch, obviously revelling in the thought of beating up the Grogs. "Ah, here's Veedor back."

The little bird she had spoken to earlier entered the room and landed beside her on the table. They exchanged words in the strange language and the bird flew off.

"Veedor has sought out the Grog fleet and says there are 23 war-boats heading at speed in the direction of Aberdod. They will be there in about five hours' time, he thinks, so you have no time to lose." She snapped at Snizu, "Prepare Zephyr 1 and Zephyr 2 for flight, immediately."

"Please, may I have my trousers back?" begged Little Dewi, at which point, the witch once more burst into uncontrollable cackling. When she had steadied herself, she waved her hand and Little Dewi's trousers rocketed into the room like a cruise missile, and shot up his

Haydn

legs so fast that he yelled in amazement as they fastened themselves around him.

They all made their way outside, to where Snizu was fitting a Krapolian saddle on Zephyr 2. The ravens looked enormous next to the little Doddies, and as they approached the birds, a sudden terrifying "Quack!" rent the air close to Little Dewi, frightening the fellow out of his skin. Out from behind a bush leapt a miniature cat, grinning broadly at the Doddies.

"Begone, Quack!" screamed the witch. The cat bounded away into a dark doorway. "He does love to wind up Doddies, knowing how you hate ducks, but the little darling is very confused. Snizu will see that you are safely mounted. I must depart now, as I have a witches' convention in Rhayader this afternoon, and I shall be demonstrating the art of Qorkinsian Spells, using a live Qork. They do love a bit of spomduffery in Rhayader, you know."

The ravens had to squat down as the Doddies mounted them. By now, Big Dewi seemed to have recovered a little. He had eaten quite a lot of *cawl* but looked quite green in the face. Snizu handed each Doddie a pair of goggles, instructing them to leave them in the saddle-bags when the ravens flew back to Plas Llanmorg. Big Dewi and Little Dewi were each fitted with a pair of antennae, which were strapped round their heads. These were used to point out to the ravens the direction in which the riders wished to fly; they extended into the raven's vision and had glowing yellow beacons on each end.

They bade Haydn farewell. He would return home by a longer and much safer route than *Llwybr-y-wrach*. With a wave, the Doddies took off, thankful to be away from that dreadful cat and glad that the earlier storm had passed. Immediately, they wheeled over the great precipice on which Plas Llanmorg stood. Zephyr 1 with Big Dewi, set course for Aberdod, and Little Dewi with Essie in the rear saddle, on Zephyr 2, headed for the Elfael Field Force headquarters, half a mile west of Bongam Bank.

Looking down, Big Dewi could see that, miraculously, *Pont-yr-ellyll* bridge had been restored to its former glory, though his head was swimming, due to the violent rocking movement of the raven. He loosened the retaining strap that Snizu had tightened to keep him in the saddle, and immediately slipped backwards. Zephyr One lurched to one side and Dewi shot forward to the limit of the strap, his feet sliding across black, shiny feathers, until he dangled over the side of the bird, the wine returning to his head as the bird side-slipped to the other side, tossing the Doddie across its neck and letting him dangle in an ungainly way on the far side. Dewi hung on, terrified, and wondered how long the strap would hold before it snapped.

6. On The Hop

"AAAEEEECHAAARRRRGGHHURRAUT!" bellowed Sergeant-Major Stadd, in a voice that sounded like a clap of thunder, and shook the assembled 2nd Light Squadron, Elfael Field Force to the core. This startled even Colonel Gnowse-Pickering, whose shack, in the shade of a large dock-leaf, stood as far away as possible from the parade ground, making him spill his gin and tonic over his jigsaw puzzle.

The scream-bellow shrieked out by the sergeant-major indicated that the assembled troopers should move forward in unison, with great haste. Although it was completely Double Dutch to anyone, especially the colonel, they all understood what needed to be done. As one, the squadron moved forward at pace, until a roar of "Aaaeeeechaaarrrrggchchurraut!" caused them to change, with absolute precision, to move backwards at the same incredible pace. It was obvious to any reasonably intelligent observer that this speed of march could not be maintained for more than two paces backwards, before they would start to fall over and end up in a chaotic heap, but the manoeuvre was in Drill Book No.132, and so it must be important. No-one dared to challenge the content of such a worthy publication.

Inevitably, the squadron ended up in a heap and slowly disentangled itself for the fourth time that week. Stadd considered it imperative in maintaining discipline, and indeed it did give him the opportunity to humiliate those he wished to bring down a peg or two. Soon, they were back on their feet, lining up and marking precise distances between themselves, as prescribed in the said drill book.

"Now, listen, you lot. They don't call me Bar Stadd for nothing! You'll get this right, even if it takes all day and all night," he chanted; this being his favourite parade-ground line. They had climbed into the saddles on their frogs and had just 'presented sabres', a move that involved six precise arm movements, when Lieutenant Lionel Lushuss arrived.

"Ewkay, men," screeched the lieutenant in his high-pitched voice. "Today we are gooooing to perfohm a two-plonged attack on the Bongam Ladies' Chuddling Club – without live ammooonishun, of cohse. It's only a plactice lun. I will lead the…" He broke off, for suddenly, with a rush of air, a huge, black bird swooped down on the assembled squadron. At the sight of this monster, they scattered in all directions; some fell off their mounts; some clung on grimly as their frogs took off in panic, whilst many went round in circles. Lieutenant Lushuss's mount threw him into a large watering trough and disappeared in a cloud of dust, much to the fellow's consternation.

Little Dewi and Essie had arrived. Flying in had been a dream. They only wished the flight had lasted longer, for they had so relished flying at tree-top height and observing all that happened below. Finding the Elfael Field Force Headquarters had been something of a problem, as even the little soldiers needed to keep hidden from inquisitive Grumpies. They flew over the area several times, trying to find a clue to the whereabouts of the squadron, and were getting rather anxious, when Essie caught sight of sunlight glinting on polished metal amidst some bushes. Down they swooped, and, to their delight, they saw the squadron practising below. Dewi did, however, forget that bringing such a large bird as a raven into close proximity with the little soldiers and their frogs might well cause havoc. Zephyr 2 squatted down and the Doddies slid off.

Dewi looked around in amazement. The carnage horrified him. Some frogs had bolted through the mess tent, causing food to be tossed around all over the place. Most troopers lay on the ground, dazed, or were picking themselves up and running off in search of their mounts, keeping well clear of the enormous bird that had parked itself on their saluting platform.

"What do you think yorrrrr doin'?" boomed the deafening tones of Sergeant-Major Stadd, as he strode up to the puzzled Doddies. "And wot's that over there?" He pointed his stick at Zephyr 2, and then waved it aggressively at Dewi. "... and who are yoooooo?" He ended with a scream that must have echoed as far as Shaky Bridge, his feet momentarily rising clear of the ground.

"I'm Dewi Bach from Aberdod, and this is my friend Essie. Just flown in on the raven – sorry about the mess, but I didn't know you were all going to panic. I thought ..."

The word 'panic' was too much for the sergeant-major. His men didn't panic. He boiled up inside, turned a bright red and thundered back at Dewi.

"Panic! My troopers do NOT panic. At the battle of Rhoscrugyceiliog, we did not panic; against the Wailing Wartcloppers, we held fast, though heavily outnumbered; and we did not flinch when attacked by hordes of Cardi pillagers. We'll see who panics! I'll have you thrown into the cooler for a day."

"Oh, please, no," Essie interrupted, alarmed at the prospect. "We mean no harm and we

Planning operations in Colonel Gnowse-Pickering's office

Twerpani roadworks holding up the cavalry squadron

only came to ask your help. We're about to be attacked by Grogs and you are our only hope."

The soldier eyed up the little Doddies with great suspicion, wondering what the horns with their flashing ends sticking out of Dewi's head might do. Dewi saw his gaze fall on the antennae and whipped them off.

"It's only flying gear," he explained. "Please help us. We haven't any time. Can I see Colonel Gnowse-Pickering?" The lieutenant had now joined them, wondering who the strangers were.

"The colonel is a very busy man, but we'll see what the he has to say," said the lieutenant. "Bling them along undah escoht." He marched off briskly in the direction of the colonel's office, followed by the others.

"Hhrrrucccccch," uttered Colonel Gnowse-Pickering, staring at Dewi through his piercing eyes, and quickly stuffing his jigsaw puzzle out of sight as the Doddies came in, flanked by the sergeant-major, who startled them by bringing his enormous boots down with a resounding crash that shook the office, causing a great cloud of dust to rise, at the same time throwing up a violent salute, to which the colonel nodded. How odd, thought Dewi. These military types behave in a most peculiar manner.

"Pardon?" queried Dewi, in answer to the colonel's strange greeting, though he was not entirely certain if it *was* meant as a greeting.

"Saaaaaahhh! Permission to speak, saaaaaah?"

Good grief, thought Dewi, wondering what all that was about. He gazed at Sergeant-Major Stadd in astonishment and caught Essie's mystified expression.

"Go on, sergeant-major."

Oh, the colonel sounded fairly civilised. The Doddies were relieved.

"Well, saaaaah, regulations clearly state

that, in a case such as this, the applicant for the assistance of an army unit should apply for the said unit, or units, on lots of complicated forms."

"Splendid, sergeant-major," remarked the colonel in his urbane accent, somewhat irritated by the extremely loud voice. He turned his gaze from the soldier to Dewi. "How exactly did you get here, little Doddie?"

"We flew here."

"Flew? You actually fly? Heavens above! Do show us."

"Well, we flew on the raven parked on your parade ground."

The colonel was astonished and took a great swig of his gin and tonic. "Is this true, Lushuss?"

Essie's eyes lifted towards the ceiling in disbelief.

"Yes, sah. They came in low over our heads and sent us pouff-ting in all dilections," replied the lieutenant.

"Remarkable. What exactly is your problem, Doddie?"

"We're about to be invaded by a Grog army, this afternoon. They intend to kill all Doddie males and run off with our women and cakes. We overheard them planning it last night." Little Dewi felt quite emotional, as he outlined their predicament.

"But, why didn't your Potchers send a

messenger with an official letter, and how did you come by the raven?"

The military seemed awfully suspicious, thought the friends.

"Because we haven't been home; we came straight here. Well, almost straight. Witch Coarsecackle leant us her raven, to get us here quickly."

The colonel's eyebrows shot up at this revelation, and he downed the remainder of his drink.

"Bit rum, this," commented the colonel. "What do you recommend, Lushuss?"

"Bit ohf the poufft for me, sah," came back the lieutenant's incomprehensible reply. "Bit fah-fetched leally. I think they're tlying to pull a jolly little pufft-tee! But it would be a jolly good old wheeze to hop down to Doddieland and duff up any Glogs we find."

The colonel snorted and wondered why he was surrounded by such idiots. True, it would be a splendid exercise, to nip down to Doddieland and get stuck into those dreadful Grogs, but if this was totally fabricated he would have more than just egg on his face. Doubt lingered though, for the Field Force had a good relationship with the Doddies, often helping them out against the wilder elements of the Howey Trolls and other dissidents. In return, the Doddies were always generous with their cakes.

"If the Grogs win," implored Essie with passion, turning on all her charms, as she racked her brains for ideas to convince the military it was vital to help, "there will be no more Doddies, no more visits by Doddie choirs, and no more Welsh cakes."

This clearly had a profound effect on the colonel. "Sergeant-major! Get Major Berk along at once, with the other officers."

"Yes, sir."

The fellow disappeared amidst a flurry of salutes and flying boots. The atmosphere instantly felt calmer to Dewi. He gave Essie's arm a grateful squeeze – she might well have saved the day. Shortly afterwards, a breathless, rather portly Major Berk arrived and joined the colonel. Time passed, with several officers hurrying to join the planning group, each carrying important-looking files, manuals, clipboards and maps. The Doddies became anxious. They thought of Big Dewi and wondered what was happening at home. Their hopes rose as the officers discussed tactics. Much

Opposite: Little Dewi and Essie on Zephyr 2 over Llandod

SPA TREATMENTS

Hydro Electric Medicated Bath
Aerated Sulphur Bath
Slag-bath Electrical Massage

The Agues, Hypochondria,
St Vitus's Dance, The Eruptions
Blushing of the Face

time was spent agreeing code-names, passwords, how much tea should be taken and asking if the Doddies would supply the cakes? Maps were pored over and plastered with arrows and crosses.

"I'd be happier with two squadrons, sir," commented Major Berk, "as there are so many Grogs. Can't we call up the 3rd Heavy Cavalry Squadron from Shaky Bridge border patrol? Their heavy toad-chariots would make short work of the Grogs."

"It would take too long," replied the colonel. "Anyway, they are guarding the border area, in case of potential uprising from that mad bunch, the Un Shoor tribe of Cefnllys. They keep changing their minds, not knowing whether to attack or not. We can't leave the border undefended. If we disappear, they'll be across Shaky Bridge in no time, looting and pillaging."

"Oh, we can poufht them Glogs by ourselves," broke in Lieutenant Lushuss boldly. Major Berk raised his eyebrows to the ceiling in frustration. He was aware that, if two squadrons were involved, Colonel Gnowse-Pickering would have to lead the attack, and he knew how much the old boy was keen to avoid battle. Far easier to stay behind, sink a few gins, and take one or two medals afterwards.

"I've dug out some catchy tunes for the lads to play," piped in Bandmaster Bumbletit. "I've just composed an especially good one for the charge – it's called 'On Llandod Moor with Big Bertha.' That'll rattle a few sabres."

The meeting droned on and on, mainly discussing irrelevant rubbish. Twice, Captain Squidge-Dunker had to be woken up out of deep slumber, and the bandmaster put outside because of his noisy and irritating habit of pretending to be a kettle-drum and banging a table rhythmically. Major Berk despaired. Eventually, the colonel drew things to a close with a stirring speech and dismissed them with: "Don't forget, I'll be right behind you!"

"Yes, miles behind us," murmured the major under his breath. "Right," this time he addressed the Doddies, "I shall be in charge of Operation Parrot Soup. We take the squadron to Aberdod, and leave as soon as we can."

Dewi jumped with delight. He knew they were unlikely to arrive before the Grogs, but, at least, if they could get home quickly on Zephyr 2, they could warn the Doddies to fall back in the direction from which the Field Force would be coming. They watched preparations. Two large guns were taken to pieces, and the barrel, wheels and mounting of each secured on a frog. A cart was loaded with ammunition and the gun crews prepared to leave. The troopers mounted their frogs, with text-book precision, and the 2nd Light Cavalry Squadron formed up in rows of three, with flags flying, drums beating, and helmets and weapons gleaming in the sunshine, as they set off at the regulation pace of 123 hops per minute cruising speed. Everything was regulated by the manual, which covered the length, height and pace of the military hop, according to close or extended order, in eleven pages with diagrams. The troopers were a splendid sight, and as they hopped down *Pant-y-gefail,* through the strange forest of Pustuled Toadstools, heading for his home, Dewi felt a tear fall. Suddenly, the soldiers stopped and stood like statues.

"Why have they stopped?" asked Little Dewi.

"They seem to have run into some road works," said Essie. "Yes, see that chap in front of them, holding up a 'STOP' board?"

"But there's nothing happening," protested Dewi. "The track is clear."

"These Twerpanis are as bad as the Grumpies, with their excessive road works" said Essie. "They just do it to annoy people … wait in ambush, they do, then jump out with their STOP signs. No reason, see. Oh, look, it's changing. He's turned the sign round to 'GET READY'. Bit of a nonsense, that."

"But he's still keeping them waiting. This is dreadful. Every minute counts and they stand there playing games." Dewi seethed with anger. "Why don't we get on the raven and give them a fright?"

Essie

"No, Dewi, that will definitely upset the soldiers." Essie looked thoughtful. "He's picking up another board, now. What does it say? 'PERHAPS?' Dewi, that board says 'PERHAPS' – are they mad?"

"This is absurd. I'm going to give them a piece of my mind." Little Dewi strode over to

Zephyr 2 and prepared to mount the raven.

"Oh no!" Essie grimaced in despair. "Hang on Dewi." She ran over to Zephyr 2 and clung to Dewi's hand, appealing to him to wait.

"Look, they're going," yelled Dewi, thankful that he didn't have to force the hand of the Twerpanis. The board now showed a large 'GO' and the soldiers once more hopped off.

Once the force was out of sight, Little Dewi and Essie settled in the saddle of Zephyr 2, and, after adjusting his goggles and antennae, Dewi gave the raven a pat, waved the antennae and, with a terrific thrust, they were airborne. Zephyr 2 climbed gradually, with a rocking motion that caused the Doddies some discomfort, but they hung on tightly, keeping the bird well to the north of the Field Force, as they saw it making its way down towards the faint shimmering of the distant lake.

They skirted round, high above the soldiers, and then set a direct course for home, gliding serenely on warm air currents. They enjoyed these moments, watching the summer countryside pass by below. To their right, they recognised Arlais Brook, where it emerged from under the trees. A group of children played on the bank. Farm-workers could clearly be seen bringing home the hay on their horse-drawn carts, and animals grazed peacefully in the meadows. How Doddies loved watching these odd Grumpies going about their business.

Zephyr 2 flew on easily, losing some height, to cruise at tree-top level. Little Dewi watched out for familiar landmarks, when, suddenly, the raven banked sharply to the right, giving them a tremendous fright. Dewi clawed with his left hand to stay upright. Out of the corner of his eye he saw two ferocious-looking crows dive down on them. Zephyr 2 banked to the left, slid under the line of approach of the crows and used its dive to increase speed. But the crows spotted this change immediately and dropped down on top of the raven. One glanced Dewi a severe blow on the right shoulder, knocking him to the left. Zephyr 2 flapped his wings to power himself out of trouble, but then hit the second crow.

This second blow, although not actually striking Dewi, caused the raven to keel over momentarily, throwing Dewi out of the saddle, as one of the straps broke. Dewi dropped like a stone, as the gallant raven battled to escape the crows. Essie gasped in horror and held on grimly, shocked that her friend had fallen out of the saddle. Desperately, she tried to look down, to see what had happened to Dewi, but trees blocked her view, as the crows attacked yet again. Tears welled up, as she felt her world falling apart. She had no antennae with which to guide the bird, so she simply tightened her grip on the saddle-handles and prayed for a safe landing.

7. Big Dewi Lands Right In It

LATELY, LIFE HAD BEEN KIND to Phergus O'Pherte. There was a spring in his step as he whistled his way towards the Doddie festivities in the Great Clearing. Phergus, who had left his native Ballyhoolydod, many years ago, to cross the Irish Sea and settle in Aberdod, where his cousin lived, had become the chief Stink-spreader. This important job involved awakening before the crack of dawn and walking around the boundary of the Doddie village, spraying a foul-smelling liquid in a continuous line all the way round. The smell would deter most wildlife, including snails, rats, cats, dogs and much more from entering Aberdod.

As the Doddies appreciated what Phergus did for them, he found that, at nearly every Doddie dwelling along his route, he was given tea and cakes, which made him extremely happy. He had attended many St Cewydd Festivals, each of which began with a procession down the lane into the Great Clearing, led by the band. Ceremonies always opened with a long sermon from the Grand Pontificator. This would be followed by speeches, then singing and dancing. The Aberdod Well-Blessing Ceremony took place just before everyone sat down for tea in the open. No one worried if it rained, as, being Doddies, they all loved wet weather.

Many stalls had been set up around the edge of the Great Clearing, selling all manner of goods and refreshments. A vast array of scrumptious Doddie cakes graced a number of stalls, from little cup cakes to mouth-watering, multi-tiered gateaux. By far the busiest stall belonged to the Prognosticator. On a day that would normally be expected to be a happy occasion, the Prognosticator, or 'Old Proggie', as he was affectionately called, raged with dire warnings of doom and gloom.

"Woe, I see naught but woe!" he wailed into the air, gesticulating wildly with his arms, to convey his sense of anguish and despair. "Such abject melancholy! Such woe! My friends, join me in my calamitous and wretched enfeeblement."

"What *is* he on about?" asked Gladys Price, a frown spreading across her face.

"I think he's … " Gwyneth began, only to

be interrupted by further wailing.

"Ooooohh, woe," chanted Old Proggie, working himself up into a fine state of pathetic misery. "We are about to receive a visitation. The skies will blacken and emit thunderbolts, flashes and bangings. Death and destruction will come raining down. The Hordes from Hell are about to descend upon us."

This took everyone aback in wonderment. Old Proggie was usually fairly accurate at foretelling events, though he often became mixed up and didn't quite get things absolutely right. Nevertheless, he was much superior to the Grumpie weather-forecasting system. People took notice and there was much muttering amongst the crowd as he continued to harangue them with fiery forecasts.

Doddies kept arriving from Llandod and the far-flung corners of Doddieland. Wild Blodwen, a curvy lady who fancied Big Dewi, flirted with a couple of the younger lads. Nearby, Major Grogbasher, a distinguished figure, nattily dressed in blazer, cravat and floral pyjama-bottoms – well, he was rather absent-minded – greeted Phergus with a wink and, "All's well and stinking, what?"

Phergus grinned. He always uttered that catch-phrase as he passed Doddie dwellings on his rounds, partly to reassure the occupants and partly to ensure a supply of cakes. The major

was really part-Twerpani, part-Doddie – true Doddies rarely displayed military characteristics.

Everyone turned out in their brightest clothes for the festival, that is, except for the Maudlin-Grommets. The Maudlin-Grommet family stood somewhat aloof from the others, dressed all in black, carrying their Doddie-bibles and looking as severe as possible. Mrs Amelia Maudlin-Grommet, a rather haughty, ugly old stick with a face that resembled a mangled turnip that had been soaked in vinegar for a fortnight, considered herself much superior to all other Doddies. Her purple nose scanned the air like some enormous, deformed radar dish, whilst her husband, equally severe-looking, kept a sharp eye on their five silent children. The large crowd now awaited the arrival of the Grand Pontificator, the Prime Potcher and Grand Lurbe, as the Llandod Close-Harmony Underwater Gargling Quintet entertained in the background.

Further up the lane, outside 'The Soggy Newt', Big Dewi's favourite pub, the band had formed up at the head of the procession. Mr Grime, the policeman, stood to attention, with his hand in the air, his brilliant red face and bulbous Doddie-nose gleaming, as he watched to see when they were ready.

"Ready, steady, GO!!!" yelled Mr Grime, at the same time dropping his arm, as though starting a race. The great drum at the rear of the band began thumping out a very fast rhythm, to which the procession was supposed to march, and as the band struck up '*The Llandod Pog-drinking Song*', they set off down the lane at top speed, Dai the drummer's long arms whacking away as fast as he could. Following the band were the girls from St Loosenuts, led by the games mistress, Martha Stiffjog, who was directly behind Dai and in danger of getting hit by his big bongers.

"Slow down, Dai Bach," yelled Dilwyn, momentarily abandoning his trumpet in desperation, "or you'll kill someone!"

Dai No-Trousers immediately took notice. His long arms stopped at the apex of their trajectory, paused, and then fell back into a slow pace – the speed of a funeral march. Several in the procession crashed into one another at the sudden pause, but because the band usually made a pretty dreadful noise, no-one seemed to notice any problems with the music.

It took some time for the band to adjust to a reasonable pace, but as they entered the Great Clearing, they looked magnificent in their plumed hats, red tunics and black polished boots. The girls of St Loosenuts stepped high and twirled their ribbons in each hand, while the Aberdod fire tender came behind, a metal watering pot with a very long spout, which the

Old Proggie

Doddies had pinched from Mrs Thomas, Ty'n y Gors. Mounted on a Doddie cart, it was towed by four Llandegley Pot-bellied Toads flanked by six orange-helmeted Doddie fire-men. The crowd cheered and the Grand Pontificator beamed broadly. Mrs Maudlin-Grommet scowled sternly ahead, until she caught the Pontificator's gaze, when she smiled weakly at him. The sun shone and there was little hint of any impending catastrophe.

Big Dewi held on grimly to the end of the saddle strap as the raven climbed into the sky, experiencing a considerable buffeting. These were terrifying moments for Big Dewi, so perhaps it was as well that he still felt a little pickled by his large intake of wine. He had never flown before and this experience was beyond his wildest nightmares. Simply getting on the bird had been traumatic, but he knew he had to do it, for his friends and family. It would have been much easier to opt out of this dreaded flight, and, equally, it seemed like madness to place himself in a position where he would most likely be attacked by hordes of Grogs, but such thoughts never entered Dewi's mind. Nothing would stop him going to the aid of his Mam and sister Gwyneth. His Dad worked many miles away, helping the Llanwrtyd Bog-Doddies to build a bog-bridging system. The Llanwrtyd branch are close cousins to the Llandoddies, and probably the most eccentric part of the greater Doddie clan. They were formed when a disgruntled family of Doddies left Aberdod and went away to hide elsewhere.

Zephyr 1 soon went into a glide as they swooped down from the higher ridge. A warm thermal gently pushed them back upwards, without any effort from the raven. He rode it for a while, soaring at times, and then gliding into a gentle dive. How Dewi hated descending; he felt so out of control. He tried to look down, with some difficulty, hanging on the strap, which miraculously held. The view stretched for miles. To the west he could see the distant lake shimmering in the sunlight. Humans could be seen working a long way below – they looked the size of Doddies, from Dewi's viewpoint. He wondered how the others were faring on Zephyr 2, then thought about his approach to Aberdod. Would he recognise the place from above and at such speed? Zephyr 1 was now flying at around tree-top height. A branch whacked against his out-turned bottom, emphasising the sense of speed. This made Dewi feel almost panic-stricken and a little sick. He hated the incessant banking from side to side, whenever the bird made slight turns to avoid obstacles.

Suddenly, from behind a large oak tree, two crows approached on an intercept course. Dewi thought nothing of it, until they closed in, looking as though they were about to attack. Zephyr 1 had spotted them early enough, and maintained course but gaining height, until the crows were almost upon them. He then banked sharply to the left, falling away at speed in a terrifying dive. Big Dewi clung on for dear life, in utter horror. "No, not that human pigsty," he thought, as they dived in a headlong rush towards a squat building. At the last moment, Zephyr 1 pulled out of the dive, turned to starboard at speed, with the crows in hot pursuit, and up past a group of tall trees, weaving in and out. Dewi felt desperately sick at being thrown around in such violent manoeuvres. The raven swept down beside a tall hedgerow, went over a garden wall and then flew beneath a washing-line. As they shot past, Dewi's antennae caught a pair of Mrs Gruffydd-Pugh's enormous knickers, and wrenched them off the clothes-line. They wrapped themselves round Dewi and his antennae. He could see nothing. They came round to the front garden, where Mrs Gruffydd-Pugh was tending her hollyhocks. She stood up just in time to see her Sunday-Best knickers fly past at speed. She fell back on her large bottom, into her compost heap, shaking her fist as her bloomers disappeared over the horizon. The crows had lost their quarry, but Zephyr 1 now had considerable problems maintaining height, with such voluminous knickers dragging him down. Gradually, the raven recovered height and resumed course for Aberdod.

Big Dewi shook with fright. The flight was proving to be as bad as his worst nightmare. He twisted round, until he was able to see through a hole in the knickers, and tried to work out if he could recognise anywhere below. Then, he looked down and saw the great metropolis of Llandrindod basking in the sunshine. He realised that they had gone too far. He lowered

The Pontificator

The Llandod Close-Harmony Underwater Gargling Quintet in action

his left antennae and Zephyr 1 banked gently to port, losing a little height as they came level with the Metropole towers. He could see lots of Grumpies down below, going about their business and taking no notice of the raven flying overhead, with a pair of extra-large bloomers billowing from its back. Oh, he could make out Mr Jones' charabanc, full of Grumpie tourists, making its way slowly towards the Pump House Hotel. Now, they were flying over the boiler house; in two minutes they'd reach Aberdod.

Dewi could recognise many places, and he caught sight of Daisy Davies, Honorary Secretary to the Doddies Eisteddfod. He waved enthusiastically at her, at which point, she dropped her tray of cakes and ran under the nearest bank. In his drunken state, he hadn't realised that, attired in the knickers, goggles and huge antennae, he resembled something from another planet. Zephyr 1 carried on past two more trees and then slowed right down and landed on a high branch of a beech tree. Dewi wondered whether it was lost, resting or awaiting orders. Should he get off? No, he decided to give the bird a gentle kick. There was no response. Perhaps it really would go no further. This was not a problem; Dewi knew he was close to his own home. But the tree was rather tall.

Dewi undid the saddle strap and slid down onto the wide branch. Giving the raven a pat and a "Thank you," he made his way along the bough, getting down on his bottom when it became too steep. All at once, he slipped, lost his grip and fell off the branch, and went crashing through dense foliage, which slowed his downward plunge. Mrs Gruffydd-Pugh's knickers billowed like a parachute, slowing his head-first dive into a moist manure heap under the tree. Dewi had landed safely, his great napper ploughing into the foul mess. With some difficulty, he extricated himself from the smelly heap and staggered across the grass to a dusty track. After pushing his goggles up and getting rid of the knickers, he could see figures in the distance and hurried after them, stinking like a skunk in a silage pit.

"Of course, it's the festival today," Dewi recalled, as he staggered into the Great Clearing. The Doddies who saw him melted away to the sides, out of the way of this strange creature. With huge strands of wet manure straggling from his two antennae, and more coming out of the top of his smock, he really appeared like something dragged out of the swamp.

"Ah, Blodwen," he yelled, as he saw his friend, but the words did not come out as usual, for the great wad of wet straw was still stuck in his mouth. Blodwen, at the sight of this awful apparition, fled down the track and out of sight. Dewi, of course, did not realise that the Old Proggie had warned of horrible things falling from the sky.

The Prognosticator was conducting an individual prognosis for Mam Jones. She had to hold a piece of dried frog manure in her clasped hands, and, with Proggie holding his hands above hers, they both looked up at the sun. On the call of "Yangacheee!" they both began simultaneously jumping up and down, still holding hands for about a minute, until Proggie yelled, "Yangachaaaa!" loudly.

"Ma'am, beware of strange horned beasts that emerge from the swamps."

"Oh dear, there's awful," Mam Jones looked alarmed, turned to go and then caught sight of Big Dewi striding towards her, with his antennae bristling. She immediately shot off as fast as her heels would carry her.

The Grand Pontificator began his sermon, working himself up to fire and brimstone, much to the delight of the Maudlin-Grommets. His black hat sat ridiculously on his enormous head, quite incapable of controlling his unkempt hair, but the most striking feature was his eye. One eye had been battered in a most unseemly disagreement with Mrs Mathias Squnch over a coffee morning presentation. This left him with one useful eye. With right arm raised, his finger wagged violently in thin air, his face black as thunder, he fired Cyclopean glares down at his audience from the stage.

"…and by the vv-u-v-verrr-ry gods that dwell on the gg-grrrr-assy slopes of Mynydd Llandod, you will r-rrr-repent your-rrr sins." His r's rolled out with great emphasis as he got into his stride, trying to overcome his stutter. He glowered down at Ianto Price, a well-known drunkard, his one functional eye almost boring holes in the chap. "At Fff-ff-ffynnon Ll-llwyn-y-gogogo they… " he paused, for the name took much energy and vast amounts of spittle, drenching those in the front row. Mrs Maudlin-Grommet glowed with pleasure. He had another go. "At Fff-ff-ff-ff… at Fff-ff-ffynon Ll-llwyn-y-gogogo they ar-rrre blaspheeeemer rr-rrs, bb-bichhots and

br rr-raddd…"

The Pontificator was at his most zealous, if sometimes totally losing his words as he heightened the pitch at the end of each sentence. Big Dewi looked up as he approached the stage. How could he interrupt this old fool? He needed to warn everyone about the Grogs.

Dewi moved forward, still unaware of the amazing spectacle he presented. He tried to brush unsteadily past some of his mates, with a wave and a "Good afternoon!" He began to climb the steps, but they grabbed him, dragged him back down, and, getting a whiff of the stench on him, pushed him away to the rear. He stumbled backwards, fighting to stay on his feet and scowling. He lurched backwards into someone: none other than Mrs Maudlin-Grommet, who screamed out as Dewi's great clod-hopper trod on her delicate foot. Dewi swung round, his left antennae knocked Mrs Maudlin-Grommet's tall hat for six. As the hat flew into the brambles, a great clod of moist manure dropped off the antennae and came to rest on the lady's brow. The sight and smell of this intolerable intrusion was too much for Mrs Maudlin-Grommet.

"Oh, Mr Maudlin-Grommet, save me from this felon," she moaned, and promptly swooned onto the grass. Big Dewi realised it was best not to hang around, and as the Pontificator had his back to him, he took a run and leapt up onto the stage, just as the Pontificator was berating the poor folk of Ffynon Llwyn-y-gog for their abysmal attendance at chapel, amongst many other sins. To everyone's astonishment, Big Dewi strode across the stage and, fortified by his tiddly condition, gave the Pontificator a forceful push, which propelled him backwards into a container of miniature nasturtiums. For a few moments, Dewi stood there, realising what he had just done. He tried to talk, but, being so unused to speaking in public, his mouth simply opened and closed like a Spondean Carp.

"Dewi – it's Dewi Mawr," exclaimed Rhiannon, who stood by the stage, feeling rather pleased that the crusty old Pontificator had shut up. "He's trying to tell us something. Talk tidy now, Dewi."

Dewi tried again, in vain. The crowd was impatient and some Doddies began to climb up onto the stage. Rhiannon ran up the steps, in her funny, lopsided way, and yelled. "Stop! It's Dewi Mawr…he's trying to tell us something important." She could read Dewi like a book, and he gave her a big hug as she came up to him. She was dearly loved by all Doddies, and despite her mental disability, which made her very slow, she was always the first to help people. She waved her arms in the air and shouted for calm.

"There's Grog boats, black boats with black sails, with hundreds of Grogs in them, and they're coming to attack us this afternoon," Dewi spoke quietly to Rhiannon.

"Listen!" Rhiannon shouted to the audience. "Dewi says there's hundreds of black Grog boats coming – nasty black boats. I don't like black. It frightens me."

"Hundreds of *Grogs*," corrected Dewi, speaking to Rhiannon, "not boats." Rhiannon looked puzzled. Dewi could see it would be difficult for her to speak for him, with her disability. He tried to speak.

"Cakes! They're after our cakes!" he stammered, gazing frantically into Rhiannon's large eyes.

"The Grogs like our cakes," she yelled at the top of her voice. "They're coming in black boats." There was a collective sigh from the assembled Doddies. Most were well aware of Rhiannon's problems. She turned to Dewi and asked, "Are the Grogs coming to our party?"

"The Grogs are coming to our party in black boats," Rhiannon shouted out excitedly, before Dewi could answer. "That will be fun!" Dewi groaned in frustration.

"They intend to attack us after tea, and take all our women away," Dewi roared out to the assembled crowd, finding his voice at last, feeling more confident with Rhiannon by his side. The audience gasped.

"Oh, there's lovely," said Mam Jones, gazing up at the stage.

Aberdod Festival in the Great Clearing

"You can't mean that," said Ceinwen. "Wicked it is, to say things like that!"

"No, no, I was talking about Rhiannon's dress – lovely pattern it is." Mam Jones lived in a world of her own.

"There's hundreds of Grogs coming," Rhiannon suddenly realised what she was saying, and held on to Dewi for comfort. She found it hard to see any wrong in people, and was always taking strangers at face value, believing everything they said. Her slowness, though frustrating to many, was more than made up for by her kindness and amazing dexterity with knitting or sewing needle, with which she was able to design and produce all manner of fashionable garments.

Dewi tore off his antennae. "The Grogs are coming! It's me – I'm here now, see?" The crowd grew hushed and sombre. The Pontificator sat amongst the nasturtiums, his one effective eye glowering, his nose a deep purple. Major Grog-basher strode over to the stage.

"Spot of trouble, eh?" he quizzed Dewi. "But you got through all right?"

"Well, we got a bit battered on the cliff," replied Big Dewi.

"Yes, I don't doubt. They don't give you a chance if they catch you unawares. Lose many chaps?"

"No, none," retorted Dewi, becoming more and more confused by the dotty old major. "But Essie was magnificent on the flying bridge."

"Flying *what?*" asked the Major, who was hard of hearing.

"Flying bridge!" yelled back Dewi, "She caught it with one hand."

"My word, what splendid chaps you have."

"Essie's a girl," protested the exasperated Dewi, relieved when others from the Potcher's Council arrived. Dewi then related the story of how they'd discovered the Grog plan and their subsequent adventures. He also told how Little Dewi and Essie had gone to ask for help from the Elfael Field Force. Gwyneth, Dewi's sister, came up and gave Dewi a hug, at last recognising him.

"Dewi, *cariad*," said Gwyneth, "lovely to see you. You're not smelling very nice, though."

"Dilwyn, send out runners at once and tell them to get as many chaps into town as they can, and to bring any weapon they can lay they hands on – hatchets and tridents if necessary," ordered the major, immediately taking charge and revelling in the thought of some action. This was *his* moment, and, perhaps, in view of his name, a preordained one. Dilwyn gathered together all the young lads he could find and sent them on their way.

"The women will have to evacuate the

place," continued the major," and get up into the hills for safety."

"Not on your life," retorted little Rhiannon, a spirited lass, despite her ailments. "Staying, we are, with the men, to help build defences. We'll get all the youngsters and elderly folk, with all the cakes, up into the old quarry, and roll rocks down on any Grogs who try to come through the narrow entrance."

"You women can't stay here," protested Will, who was one of the potchers. "You heard what Dewi said – the Grogs will take you away – if you don't get killed in the process."

"We're staying!" growled Blodwen, as she and several women ganged up on Will.

"Will's right, if we all leave, they can't harm us," added Big Dewi, "then, when we…"

"Rubbish," snorted Martha. "We're staying. I'm not having Grogs running riot in my home. We're going to defend Aberdod to the last."

The major knew he would not win that argument, so he gave further orders. "We'll build a barricade around the main area, and try to hold out till the Elfael chaps get here. Use anything you can lay your hands on. I'll get out my field piece and give it a good servicing."

At this, the Doddies groaned. Major Grog-basher's old artillery piece was extremely erratic, its cannon-balls rarely hitting the intended target. He practised with it, every now and

then, and usually blew up something.

Dewi watched the major issuing orders right and left, and realised that the old fool had no hope of turning the Doddies into a fighting force. They simply wouldn't stand a chance against the highly-aggressive Grogs. It would be far better to abandon the place, leave the cakes to the Grogs and return with the Elfael Field Force, but the Doddie women had no intention of leaving, and so there was nothing for it but to fight to the end.

The Soprano Gargler

8. The Grogs Attack

ABERDOD BUZZED WITH ACTIVITY as work began on the defences. Stakes were driven into the mud and banks, and all kinds of obstacles, weird and wonderful, dragged out to fill any gaps. Mam Jones brought out her heavy mangle and Nigel Withering-Bottom worked wonders with an old bedstead and some string. Boulders and large tree branches were rolled into position, to defend behind, and smaller ones were to be thrown down onto the invaders. A deep ditch was dug behind the barricade, to put the attackers at a disadvantage. Spears were fashioned, and anything that could be used as a weapon was brought into use. Daisy, especially, made remarkably imaginative use of her kitchen utensils.

The unwarlike Doddies found all this sort of activity quite alien, but Major Grog-basher performed sterling work in organising matters. Once everyone had been set tasks, the major wheeled out his ancient field piece and pointed it towards the corner from which he felt the Grogs were most likely to approach. With the aid of two Doddies, he stood the gun in a shallow depression and placed the cannon-balls

nearby. Then, as he began polishing his helmet, which was actually made out of a brass thimble, old Mrs Squnch walked past.

"Playing soldiers again, is it, Mr Grogbasher?" she mocked the major, who ignored the old stick, knowing how she loved to argue, sometimes violently. She continued in a huff.

Gradually, the Doddie numbers swelled. Lewis Lewis, one of the few Doddie farmers, arrived with his hybrid muck spreader drawn by two mice. It gave a somewhat erratic performance, being difficult to aim. Lewis had filled it up with the foulest manure he could find, and laced it with lethal rocks. Shortly afterwards six Doddie frog-tamers ran in, having heard the news. Mr Fusspot, the Prime Potcher, greeted them warmly and passed them on to the major for orders. Ifan Gof, the blacksmith, fashioned spears and tridents as fast as he could, and Evan Nant-y-Ddwy Cawrfil arrived with his two sons, all carrying huge axes.

"Good Man," beamed the Potcher, his eyes moist with gratitude. "The women are doing really well. Not only have they organized refreshments by the stage, but Gladys Price has got them boiling great vats of custard, to drop on the Grogs from the top of *Craig-y-moch*. Martha is getting her friends to create a last-ditch defence in the old quarry, and taking all the youngsters and infirm up there, out of the way. We'll show them Grogs what we're made of."

In the meantime, the two groups of Doddies intended for the counter-attack were practising in the Great Clearing. Sadly, it became rather chaotic, and ended up as a general free-for-all.

"Look you, Dai Bach, no need to hit so hard; it's only practice," complained Dilwyn, as the pint-sized drummer rained blows on the unfortunate chap who had fallen to the bottom of the mêlée. It took some time for them to extricate themselves, and Mr Grime, who was trying to maintain some degree of order, dragged them apart. This did not augur much hope for success in the forthcoming battle.

"We're not doing very well here," said Mr Grime, in a low voice, to the Potcher, as he was making his rounds. "This lot are in a chaotic state; there's not enough of us to defend the whole perimeter; we have few effective weapons; and the major thinks we can conquer the world. Well, he's in for a disappointment."

Mr Grime had always been down-to-earth, a backbone of Doddie society, if a trifle pessimistic. Mr Fusspot could see that this episode was affecting him badly.

"Keep spirits up, old friend," he said quietly, but firmly, putting a comforting hand on Grime's shoulder. "Things are never as bad as they seem. Oh, Mrs Maudlin-Grommet, may we have a word?"

Amelia Maudlin-Grommet, had recovered from her earlier ordeal and was searching for one of her daughters, when the Potcher spotted her passing.

"I have a little task for you," the kindly Potcher said, trying to be as diplomatic as possible, aware of Mrs Maudlin-Grommet's fragile state of mind.

"I don't do *taaasks,* Mr Fusspot," she retorted sharply, her nose high in the air as she sailed on without pause.

"Tell me, how many of those delightful hats do you possess?" Mr Fusspot asked.

Mr Fusspot tried hard to keep up with her. The severe-looking frown on her face turned to puzzlement at this strange question.

"Why, Mr Fusspot, I have 52 in my collection," she replied, drawing a wry smile, to indicate her satisfaction at being able to show how well off she was. Most Doddies owned just one hat or cap. "One for each Sunday in the year."

"My word, Mrs M, that's amazing! Tell me, are they all the same?"

Approach of the Grogs

"Precisely and exactly the same, Mr Fusspot, the tallest I could find," confirmed the redoubtable lady, positively beaming with pride at discovering this unexpected interest in her outstanding wardrobe. Little did she realise that the Potcher pondered, in utter disbelief, why she would need 52 black hats, all exactly the same. "Will that be all?"

"Well, I was wondering if you would help us out with a slight problem," said the Potcher, taking her by the arm and swinging her in the direction of her home.

Mr Grime gazed at the pair in astonishment as they set off; their conversation was soon out of earshot, though he heard her startled comment, "Really, I'm not sure what Sidney would think of this if he finds out."

Time was passing. Would their defences be ready in time for the arrival of the Grogs? The hot July sunshine beat down on the war-boats that ploughed across the lake. Ongut had given orders that no boat was to stop in open water, in case of underwater attack by Doddies. They constantly searched the water ahead for coracles, but saw only empty space. Of the four captured Doddies, Iestyn suffered worst, at the hands of Igrun, a huge beast of a Grog, who caught Iestyn by the throat and shook him like a doll, while he was tied up on the deck.

"When we land, red Doddie, you'll guide us to the back of Aberdod, where we'll surprise them. Tell me: how many male Doddies live there?" As he asked the question, Igrun brought his great knee down on Iestyn's chest, forcing the breath out of him. Iestyn spluttered in agony.

"I can't count more than nine," he croaked, when the giant Grog eased off his chest. With a cruel slash, Igrun hit him across the face and repeated the question. Several times he was beaten in this way, until, in the end, he saw it would be best to give some figure, way below the actual number.

"There's about 132 male adults," he offered, but this didn't seem to convince the Grog, who hit him even harder.

"I want the true figure," he roared, grasping Iestyn once more around the neck.

"But, that is the true fi …"

This time, Iestyn reeled from a terrific blow, which jerked back his head and hit it against the hard deck. At that point, he gave in and told the Grog everything that he wanted to know.

Not long afterwards, the fleet turned north-east. With a slight adjustment of direction, they glided into a small bay, where the shore was heavily wooded. The boats grounded and were dragged ashore. Stores were unloaded, whilst a council of war was held by the leaders.

"We're close to Aberdod," said Ongut, now dried out from his several wettings. "To catch them by surprise, we'll march from here and attack on two sides. Our red-haired friend has supplied information, and this has been confirmed by what Leila has gleaned from the young one. As we begin our assault, six boats will bombard the shore area and sink any Doddie vessels that try to flee.

"Igrun, you will lead the group attacking from the rear. Take the red-haired Doddie with you, to show you the way, and keep those females under control. Alfar, you will lead the group attacking along the shoreline. The young Doddie will go with you. I'll command the bombardment vessels. The other boats will remain drawn up on the shore, under guard."

"Leading from the rear, are you, Ongut?" taunted Leila, as she rubbed oil into her arms.

Ongut, noticeably twitching, fought back his rage and turned a blind eye to her taunts. Most of the warriors were painting red and yellow marks across their faces, to make them look even more ferocious.

"There will probably be no resistance – they don't even know we're coming. Right now, they are probably digging into their afternoon tea. They won't know what's hit them!" Ongut was buoyant and spoiling for a fight. "We don't need the archers, so they can stay and guard the boats. Anyway, last time, I got an arrow right in the backside from that lot. 'Friendly fire,' I think the Grumpies call it. Grogs! Let's go! Gra-Gra-Grog! Gra-Gra-Grog!"

At the terrifying Grog war-cry, off they went, so eager that they jostled to be at the front. Alfar led one group and Igrun the other. Their weapons glinted in the sunlight as they moved fast but silently through the trees. The Grog warriors were clad in spiky armour, thirsting for action, and not doubting victory for one moment. It would be difficult to see how the unwarlike Doddies could survive against such a formidable force. Not only were the Doddies no match for these warriors, but they were also heavily outnumbered. With the groups went a band of female Grogs, led by Leila, determined to show their male counterparts that they could fight just as well. Leila had her own agenda, with dreams of overthrowing Ongut as Grog leader. The battle was about to start.

With the crows attacking ferociously, Zephyr 2 battled to stay airborne, jinking one way, then another, which terrified Essie. The raven pulled up just before it hit a tree, then flew around it and under the foliage of a thick blackthorn, to confuse the crows and make its escape. At this point, several pigeons panicked at the disturbance and flew off in all directions, causing the crows to lose contact. After a few moments, Essie, still strapped securely in her saddle, realised that they had been shaken off, but she still sobbed at the thought that she'd lost Little Dewi.

She had no idea where they were, and really wanted to get off the raven as soon as possible. Suddenly, she caught sight of the Great Clearing, with many Doddies milling about. How could she tell Zephyr 2 to land immediately? She poked his back and tried to indicate with her arm, but it wasn't long enough. After a few moments, Essie removed her belt and dangled it as far forward as possible, hoping the raven would think she wanted to go straight down.

Zephyr 2 obliged without hesitation, diving steeply in a curving descent that brought them down into a small clearing in the wood. He landed with a hop, and squatted down so that Essie could dismount. She slid onto the soft grass and thanked the bird. She looked around for a clue as to her position, but not recognising any landmark, felt completely lost. She only had a vague idea of her position, and moved off quickly to where she thought she might find Aberdod, working her way through the trees.

Back in Aberdod, preparations continued. Deep holes had been dug under the trees, where they were difficult to spot, and covered with light branches and vegetation. The major marched back and forth amongst the various groups of Lilliputian defenders, trying to keep up morale, and, in the background, the Doddie choir was giving a rousing rendition of 'Men of Harlech.' They were supported by the Llandod Close-Harmony Underwater Gargling Quintet who, alas, had some difficulty with prolonged gargling above water, especially at the frenetic pace of 'Men of Harlech'.

Most of the Doddies were silent, listening for the merest crack of a twig to betray the presence of the enemy. Little Iolo Price stood high on the tallest crag, and gazed out across the lake, in search of the Grog fleet. He and his mother, Gladys, were actually Gooey Doddies from Builth, and were only visiting Gladys's cousin, Ceinwen. 'Gooey' is a corruption of the word 'Gwy,' the Welsh name for the river Wye. Gladys kept the fires burning, to simmer the custard that would be dropped onto any Grogs who appeared below the crag that she and her friends occupied. It couldn't be long now. They all prayed that Little Dewi would get through with the Elfael Field Force as soon as possible. Big Dewi, now recovered from his drunken state, stood chatting to Wild Blodwen. They were playfully pretending to hit each other.

Beneath a towering ash tree, Will Pant-y-Felin dozed in the afternoon heat. He was not the best of sentries; he had been celebrating St Cewydd's Day in the 'Soggy Newt', at lunchtime. Suddenly, a sharp crack woke him up. Startled, he gazed around for any sign of others. More sounds reached him, as though a number of people were trying to move quietly through the wood. Dark, moving heads appeared, mysteriously cloaked in the dark undergrowth. Then, he recognised the figures that stretched across the front for as far as he could see. "Grogs!" he whispered to himself, his heart beating fast. Will shot up, gave three loud blasts on his horn, and set off in the direction of his friends, fleeing as though a veritable army of bloodthirsty geese were after him.

Near the shoreline, the commotion in the trees warned the Doddies that something nasty might be about to happen. Shortly afterwards, scores of Grogs burst out of the woods and

Major Grogbasher prepares his field piece

raced across the shallow stream, yelling their war-cries, "Gra-Gra-Grog!" The water slowed them a little before they climbed up the far bank, where Big Dewi and his friends awaited the onslaught. The sight of so many dark, aggressive Grogs, waving their swords and baring their teeth, absolutely petrified the Doddies. They had never before met anything like this onslaught from the most hideous creatures imaginable. How long would the barricade hold? At the front came the giant Alfar, roaring and spitting. He stopped by the barricade, beat his chest, picked up the tree trunk that had been intended to serve as the main part of the barricade, and tossed it to one side as though it were a piece of straw. The Doddies gasped – it had taken six of them to drag that trunk into position.

Alfar grasped Mrs Jones' mangle, twisted the metal into a ball and hurled it at the defenders. He then sent three Doddies reeling, as he advanced with his fellow warriors. Some leapt over the barricade as though it weren't there, but many Grogs stumbled over it. Some fell into the ditch, some didn't. Some leapt so high over the barricade that they fell straight into the ditch.

Big Dewi saw the danger from the giant Grog who was now demolishing poor old Mr Grime. Across the clearing charged Dewi, roaring like a bull, his head down. His famous

napper hit Alfar right behind the knee. The Grog instantly crumpled, crashing to the ground with such force that it vibrated across Aberdod. Blodwen, following up behind Dewi, flung a fish net over the fallen Grog and hit him between the eyes with a metal bar she'd found. Two more Doddies seized the moment to rain more blows down. More nets and ropes quickly stopped his struggles, and he was dragged into the bushes.

More Grogs broke through the gap in the barricade. Dewi prodded one with his long-handled trident, spinning him round and presenting Blodwen with a large bottom, into which she sank the garden fork with all her might. The Grog screamed, bolted into the woods, clutching his bottom, and was never seen again.

All along the line, the Doddies were trying to prod the Grogs back into the stream with their longer tridents. The attackers were clearly surprised by this stout and ready defence, when they expected the Doddies to be sitting around, drinking tea. Fresh Grogs leapt out of the trees, one group aiming for a point where the Doddie line was at its thinnest. Several Doddies lost their tridents, as the Grogs grabbed them and pushed them back across the clearing. On the left flank, the Grogs began to overwhelm the defenders, who broke and ran back towards Major Grogbasher. Lewis Lewis saw the danger and, urging his mice on, raced across the front of the line, spraying the Grogs with a lethal mixture of manure and rock. Unfortunately, in order to spray out its cargo, his muck-slinger had to keep moving, and so several Doddies became doused in the potent mixture. Will Pant-y-felin groaned when he caught a generous serving of manure in the face, while Fergus, luckily, bent over to dodge a Grog sword just as a full fusillade shot past, demolishing three Grogs. Alas, Fergus was immediately deluged with a further shower of muck and stones.

The major's moment had come, as the Grogs hesitated after their dusting from Lewis. "Fire!" he roared. His field piece belched out flame and a great black cloud of smoke. Although it was vaguely pointing in the direction of the Grogs, the cannon-ball whistled across the Great Clearing and hit the starboard rear wheel of Lewis's muck-slinger, instantly reducing it to matchwood.

Lewis cursed. "That barmy major and his damned cannon! Just as I was starting to enjoy it."

There was no time to repair the machine, but Lewis gallantly hauled the thing round through 180 degrees and set off back at speed on three wheels, to give the Grogs another pasting. As he tore past for the second time, the major's second cannon-ball was on its way.

It is said that lightning never strikes twice in the same place, but, clearly, no-one had told Lewis. With an almighty crash, the missile took away Lewis's other rear wheel, completely wrecking any chances of further fusillades from the brave farmer.

"Shiverin' squits! Which side is that old fool on?" Lewis was now beside himself with rage, fuming, cursing and waving his fist at the major. It was as much as Ifan Gof could do to stop Lewis rushing over and giving Major Grogbasher a poke. A Grog hit him, and Lewis set about them with his pitchfork. Several Grogs had crashed into the pits dug by the Doddies, but as they hadn't dug them very deep, the Grogs simply heaved themselves out and continued the battle. Some booby-traps worked, but there were simply too many Grogs. Gwyneth ran up to the major.

"Mrs Maudlin-Grommet told me to tell you that she is ready. When do you want her to start?"

"Damn it… I'll wave my hand," said the major in exasperation. "I've only got three balls left, you know!"

"Oh, really, major," said an expasperated Gwyneth, and ran off.

The major loaded one of his few cannon-balls, and then he noticed the six Grog bombardment vessels sailing across the front of the shoreline where the Great Clearing ran down to the lake.

"Oh no, this is going to be a massacre," he said, dragging the gun round to engage the boats. As he did so, the boats opened up with rocks, which they catapulted into the clearing. They were pretty inaccurate, but with so many missiles in the air, they were bound to hit something. One landed close to the gun, drenching the major and his crew with earth and stones. Another demolished the stage with all its festive decorations. Yet another landed on the unfortunate muck-spreader, sending manure flying in all directions, hitting Grog and Doddie alike, and totally demolishing the machine. Lewis watched in disbelief, as his muck-spreader blew up with spectacular effect. There was a delay of a second or two, then, clenching both fists and incandescent with rage, he began waving them at Major Grogbasher, who quickly retreated. The major's helmet fell off as he rapidly retired backwards.

"You blithering idiot," roared Lewis, raving and shaking his fist at the helmet with unrestrained rage. He grabbed a huge axe and proceeded to smash the major's helmet to smithereens, every now and then pausing, to wave a fist at it and curse its dubious parentage.

"Take that, you … you mangled pile of maggot's brains. With a whack, he brought the axe down again, severing the remains of the helmet in half, then almost gleefully stamping on it. The major nervously observed this performance from a safe distance.

Six Doddies fled in the face of another ferocious Grog attack. The main line was breached. The remainder fell back towards the centre of the clearing, in complete confusion, many running round in circles, in disarray. Dewi saw the danger. As seven or eight Grogs rushed forward, he tore into them single-handedly. Sidney Maudlin-Grommet gazed in awe at the Doddie's amazing disregard for his own safety. Again, Dewi's head met a Grog stomach, and the creature fell pole-axed, taking two of his friends with him. Another Grog howled in agony, when Dewi's trident found his enormous snout. As the remainder came on, one of Ongut's missiles crashed down on top of them and bounced through several more Grogs. Ongut hadn't adjusted his aim to account for the rapid advance. Big Dewi jubilantly waved his trident in the air, as he routed so many of the enemy. Several defenders joined him and put their trusty tridents to good effect. By now, sadly, a great number of Doddies had been caught and taken prisoner. At this moment, the inland section of the Grog force, led by the notorious Igrun, emerged from the trees below the cliff to the left of the action. If it succeeded in joining up with the other Grogs it would cut off the main Doddie defenders' escape route.

Dilwyn and the few lads holding the left

The Battle of Aberdod

flank stood transfixed as the Grog horde raced towards them, chanting "Gra-Gra-Grog! Gra-Gra-Grog!" They could never hold out against this lot. Two of the Doddies had bows and arrows, and let fly, dropping two or three Grogs as they stormed out of the undergrowth beneath *Craig-y-moch*.

"Now, girls," yelled Gladys Price, with venom in her voice for once. Over went the great vats of boiling custard, together with several boulders, and landed on top of the Grog band. With yells of anguish, they leapt back into the stream and rolled around in the water, roaring like demented bulls.

"Yes, we've got 'em. Put the next lot of custard on."

Dilwyn could hardly believe his luck. For a moment, the threat from that quarter was stopped, but more Grogs were building up on the other side of the stream and working their way round, out of range of the custard-hurling women. It could only be minutes before they completely over-ran the defenders.

With the help of his eccentric assistant, Funkum Spratt, and the Doddie twins, Branwen and Bronwen, Doctor Phatbellie had set up a first aid station near the entrance to the quarry. Thankfully, casualties so far amounted to just a few broken limbs, bruises and headaches, thanks to the tridents keeping the Grogs at a distance. This state of affairs couldn't last much longer, and the doctor expected fatalities to begin soon. Bald as a coot, with a few straggly hairs, he calmly went about his business, bandaging and dispensing potions to his casualties. His brightly-coloured potions, which were all identical apart from their colour, were very popular. After diagnosis, he asked his patients which colour they preferred, and dispensed accordingly. Bandages were similarly varicoloured, and fashion-conscious patients could co-ordinate them with their clothing.

The Grand Pontificator busied himself by going around those who had been hurt, and relayed messages between the several Doddie groups. Several Doddies were missing, but most had regrouped and formed a semi-circle around the major and his gun.

After a while, Essie saw occasional glimpses of the lake glistening through gaps in the trees. The sound of fighting in the distance was getting louder. She felt sick. Was this the end of Aberdod and all her friends? She felt emotions rise inside her – and despaired at the thought of what these fiends were doing. This changed to anger and a determination to do what she could to hurt the Grogs. She found it hard to concentrate. She remembered that some of the Grogs had planned to attack near the shoreline, so she moved further inland, in the hope of sneaking into Aberdod from round the back,

Grogbasher

and joining her friends. The Grogs were making a dreadful noise and so she confidently expected to avoid them.

Soon, she could make out dark, evil-looking shapes moving quickly through the undergrowth. "Grogs!" she gasped. Although expecting them, the sight of them, evil and sinister in their body armour, made her pulse pound. The adrenalin kicked in and she moved away further inland. Hardly had she gone ten paces, when more Grogs burst out of the trees on the opposite side. She panicked and turned back the way she had come, but it was too late: the Grogs had seen her. They gave chase, but were slowed down by their body armour, and she out-ran them. Then, on the point of getting away, she tripped on a root and fell heavily on her side. Winded, she rose and found a third group of Grogs almost upon her.

Essie gallantly started off to the left and deftly evaded a couple of warriors, but the third grabbed her. She kicked him on the shin and he hopped around for a few moments, but another Grog caught her and picked her up as though she was a feather. She kicked, bit and struggled in vain, until the Grog shoved her head inside a bag of fish-bait. She found herself flung into a large net, along with seven other captured Doddies. The net shot up and was hung unceremoniously in a bush. She ripped the bag off her head, and, from her uncomfortable position, she could see many other nets, each containing scores of Doddie prisoners. Her heart sank. Despite all their efforts, the Doddies were being overwhelmed by these awful creatures.

Meanwhile, in the woods further north, Leila and her heavily armed band of female Grogs skirted to the east of the main action. They reached the crags, which here were fairly easy to climb, unlike the cliffs below Gladys Price. Stealthily, the female band scrambled up, watching for any sign of Doddies. At the top, they pushed through thick vegetation, and then Leila signalled them to stop.

"Look girls," she pointed, "the Doddies have put their old folk, women and kids in the quarry down there. A piece of cake!"

9. Fireworks

Lieutenant Lushuss raised his right arm and brought the forward troop to a halt. "Ten minutes to watah yoh flogs," he proclaimed, then dismounted and led his frog down to the water's edge. Major Berk drew up beside him.

"We're now at Twll Du, so we must have about an hour to go, before we reach the outskirts of Aberdod. Looking forward to a decent scrap, what?"

"Yes, sah!" exclaimed the lieutenant, trying to sound enthusiastic, although a scrap was the last thing he fancied. His earlier enthusiasm had dissolved. He glanced skywards. "Good day foh it!"

"Twerp," thought the major, not entirely convinced by Lushuss and his affected manner of speaking. "Ah, what's this?"

A trooper with a bunch of feathers in his hat, indicating he was with the signals unit of 2nd Squadron, ran up. With a quick salute he addressed the lieutenant.

"Sir, message from one of the forward flying pickets. He's heard a number of explosions from the direction of Aberdod."

Messages were flashed for some distance by a series of mirrors.

"Go-osh!" said the lieutenant. "That must mean the battle has begun. It'll be all ovah by the time we get theh. Buglah, sound the owdah to mount."

Many of the frogs took exception to being dragged away from the water so quickly, and needed some handling. Soon, the squadron was on its way once more, but, even at the regulatory 123 hops per minute, they did not hold out much hope of reaching Aberdod in time to save the Doddies.

Back in Aberdod the battle still raged. Leila and her female warriors fixed ropes made of Grumpie thread attached to heather branches and used them to abseil down the cliffs into the quarry. Their stealth had paid off, for, as yet, no-one had seen them. Leila went first, dropping over the top of the cliff and smoothly bouncing her way down on the rope, followed by the others, eight at a time. They tried to keep as silent as possible, to maintain surprise, but very quickly they were spotted. Old Elfyn,

Funkum Sprat fits a Clockwork Rejuvenating Corset on to Lewis Lewis

who suffered from many ailments, which often took all afternoon to discuss with his friends, happened to be looking towards the cliff. At 221 years of age, his eyesight could not be said to be at its best, so he was not sure precisely what he was seeing.

"Look you," he exclaimed excitedly to his friends, "there's teddy-bears running down the cliff!"

"Don't be silly," challenged Mrs Squnch, who sat nearby, trying to work out a crossword puzzle. She took great delight in disagreeing with everyone, and, indeed, had laid out the Pontificator with a left hook on at least one occasion, and was responsible for his loss of one eye. "You youngsters are all the same. Impertinent little jumped-up pratts. Why don't you do something useful, like stick your head in a jar of marmalade?" She chortled loudly. Bright as a spark was Mrs S, even though she was at least thirty years older than Old Elfyn, and getting ruder with every year that passed.

"No, seriously – there's lots of 'em, waving their arms about and bouncing around. Look up there, you old faggot."

"Don't you faggot me, you old crow!" Mrs S stood up and gave Elfyn's rocking chair such a push that he began rocking down a slope in the direction of the female Grogs, who had already landed at the bottom of the cliff. Several of the Doddies looked up, to see Old Elfyn rattling down the slope, and then they caught sight of the Grog intruders.

"Get help, Gwyneth," yelled Martha Stiffjog, who was in charge of the elderly, spotting the second group of Grogs abseiling down the cliff. Martha ran around, yelling at the top of her voice. Gwyneth headed off towards the Great Clearing.

Leila gathered together her band, until she had enough to mount an attack. She witnessed the commotion caused by Old Elfyn, but knew it was pointless to go into action with only a few warriors. Then, the Grog females advanced across the quarry floor, past fallen boulders. Martha dragged Elfyn back to safety, with the aid of two other girls, and she and several others formed a line between their charges and the Grogs. Armed only with a motley collection of rolling pins, brooms, spades and the like, they hoped help would soon arrive. Mam Jones gripped her washing dolly tightly and was confident that she would knock out several Grogs with it.

To a yell of "Gra-Gra-Grog", the Grogs waded into the attack. Leila stood head and shoulders above the others. Her sword flashed in the sunlight and demolished Mam Jones's washing dolly with one blow. Mam Jones quickly turned on her heels and ran. Leila sent two more Doddie ladies flying. Martha hurled a net over a couple of Grogs, who became tangled up and fell over, only to be replaced by three more Grogs, snarling menacingly. A custard pie hit one of them in the face, with the heavy earthenware dish still attached. Martha's aim was pretty hot, as she played left stunker in the Doddie ladies' ibgur team, and quickly despatched a second Grog, courtesy of a rhubarb tart with rum and cinnamon flavouring.

Still the Grogs forced their way forward, as Doddies strove to avoid the blows raining down on them. Nigel Withering-Bottom ran up from the direction of the clearing, confident that he would soon sort out these Grog ladies. Smash! A Grog fist caught him a pile-driver on the jaw, and he collapsed to the ground. Luckily for Nigel, the Grogs were too busy to stick any swords in him. Martha glanced at his prone figure and thought it very odd that they didn't finish him off. They seemed to be able to leap over boulders with the greatest of ease, making defence difficult. One of them reached Mrs Squnch, who, despite her 251-plus years, began wrestling and punching in a most aggressive manner. Together, they rolled over and over, with the ancient Mrs S yelling obscenities, as they kicked, scratched and poked each other in the eye. She was a wily old bird, and soon prostrated her opponent by rolling on top of her and pinning her down with her enormous bottom – the largest in Doddieland. While Mrs S sat on the Grog, she secured her to the ground by thrusting knitting needles through her body-armour links. Despite this, it could now only be minutes before the gallant Doddie ladies would be put to flight. Rhiannon could see things getting grim, and tried to herd the children up the slopes, to hide them in the vegetation, out of the way. The St Loosenuts' schoolgirls, however, had other ideas and began to assail the Grog females with fusillades of stones and stale Welsh Cakes – from a distance. Typically, Rhiannon took care of the little ones single-handedly.

Off-shore, the bombardment resumed, raking the shoreline. One lucky shot from the *Brecon Tart* crashed into Major Grog-basher's gun and knocked the barrel off its carriage, disabling the piece completely. This action might well have been of advantage to the Doddies. Ongut was jubilant. He danced a jig on the prow of the *Brecon Tart,* as he could see his warriors winning the battle. The Doddies looked done for, in spite of Big Dewi's magnificent efforts. Another rock was heaved onto the catapult, and Ongut bent down to kiss it. Unfortunately, the Grog operating the trigger didn't notice this, and as he fired the missile, it caught Ongut a whack across the right ear, sending him flying into the lake. This did nothing to improve his temper.

Grogs were pressing along the shoreline and up towards the quarry entrance. The Doddies, outnumbered and outclassed, fought a brave battle but were now tiring rapidly. One Grog, caught in an elasticated worm-trap, spun around 270 times in two minutes and then hung from a bush like a mangled daffodil. Lewis Lewis had been knocked out by a glancing blow from a club, and Funkum Spratt, the doctor's assistant, was trying to fit one of the doctor's Clockwork Rejuvenating Corsets (patent pending) on him, but had great difficulty in finding one large enough to go round Lewis. The two nurses were bandaging as fast as they could, but casualties were mounting. As the Grog line drew closer, the doctor asked that the first aid station be moved up into the quarry, and the more badly injured Doddies had to be carried up.

In front of the cake stalls, several Grogs surged forward, led by the ferocious Grog with huge dreadlocks. He'd spotted the jellies, ranged in all colours and flavours on the stall, and couldn't wait for the battle to end so that he could begin stuffing them till he was sick. Alas, the first aid station stood between him and his beloved jellies. Here lay many Doddies, injured and defenceless, being tended by the nurses, the Pontificator and others. Bronwen looked up and saw the Grogs rushing straight towards her. Her piercing scream could be heard above the sounds of battle, causing Big Dewi to glance round as he demolished another Grog.

"Oh, Bron," he muttered, and raced to intercept the Grogs, but he was too slow. Desperately, he hurled his axe, which he'd traded for his broken trident. Dewi wasn't the best of throwers. The axe, aimed at the Rastafarian Grog, sailed high into the air, curved well away from its intended target and came down with an almighty crash on Mrs Crumb-Potty's Steam-driven Cake-Mixing Apparatus. This incredible device was invented by Professor Megawattie.

The axe hit the steam-release pipe, denting it badly and preventing excess steam escaping. Quickly, this built up pressure inside the boiler, which began to shake violently. Next to the boiler, the hot batter for pancakes had started to sizzle, when the boiler exploded suddenly, showering the on-coming Grogs in thick, sticky and revolting batter. Bronwen watched all this in amazement. The Grog hordes were blinded, frantically trying to pick off lumps of solidifying batter from their faces and hands. They stood helpless, unable to see anything, many falling over the others in their panic. Big Dewi took the opportunity to despatch well over twenty Grogs with a heavy spade he picked up, whacking them mercilessly. Singlehanded, he had saved the first aid post, but still the Grog masses rushed forward, and Dewi could not be everywhere.

Gryphor was elated, as he hacked the end off another Doddie trident with his huge sword. "We have them, we have them! They are done for now."

His black eye and bleeding nose simply added to his disgusting appearance. Forward he strode, pausing only to grab a honey-doughnut off Mrs Jones' cake-stall, before continuing to hack at the retreating Doddies. More Grogs poured out of the trees. They came along beneath the cliffs and grouped, with shields and branches held aloft, to fend off Gladys' custard and boulder pummelling. Some were so covered in mud and slime that they looked as though they'd crawled out of a swamp. They waded in from the bombarding boats, all along the shore, and they raced across the stream. There seemed no end to them, as they forced the tired Doddies back. In the quarry, more of Leila's girls abseiled down the rock face. Things, indeed, looked bleak for the Doddies. Never in their history had they been subjected to anything as violent and devastating as this. Many were now in a bad way, suffering from severe cuts and bleeding. Some had lost consciousness. The remaining Doddies backed towards the quarry entrance, fending off the Grogs with their tridents.

Sidney Maudlin-Grommet, as he threw stones at the enemy, found himself suddenly flattened by an aggressive warrior, and only in the nick of time did Big Dewi rescue him, by sending the Grog flying with a ferocious head-butt. Dewi inspired the defence – in fact, it would all have been over by now if he had not been there. Dewi's heroic actions made him a marked target, and when he slipped, several Grogs leapt on him, to Blodwen's dismay. She had performed magnificent work with her garden fork, but now she leant, weeping, against the cliff. Gwyneth put her arm around her.

"Perhaps the Elfael soldiers will arrive soon," she tried to comfort Blodwen. "Gosh – why is Funkie talking to that Grog?" Funkum Spratt stood in a shadowy cleft in the cliff, earnestly discussing something with a ferocious-looking Grog. After a few moments, they parted and moved away in different directions.

"That's very strange, Gwyn. What's he up to? Is he friendly with these monsters, then?" Blodwen wiped away her tears. "Sorry, Gwyn, I can't let Dewi see me like this. I'm shattered. This is the end for all of us. I can't see us getting out alive. Whenever Dewi knocks one down, three more Grogs appear."

Smoke drifted across the clearing, as the Grogs set fire to stalls, homes and people's property. Some were already looting, as they sensed victory. Few Doddies now remained fighting, as the battle focussed on the narrow quarry entrance. Even Gladys's girls, who rained down rocks on the massed Grogs, were losing heart. They were rapidly running out of rocks. The major, wounded in one leg, sat yelling encouragement nearby, but he, too, was demoralised. Bronwen and Branwen sobbed uncontrollably, as the Doddie injured cried for help.

All of a sudden, there came a tremendous Swooooosssshh, a clap of thunder and a deafening cackle. "Aaaaaaach…aha aha ha ha ha ha ha ehe ehe he he he he!!!" The sky darkened but, to Dewi, the noise was unmistakeable.

Witch Coarsecackle roared past on her *Sky-Scimitar-6* broomstick, red, white and green thunderbolts firing out of her wand, as she directed it at the Grogs. In a blue flash, the Grog swords and spears turned into miniature bananas, and momentarily the warriors froze, completely baffled. Gryphor swung back his arm, to bring his sword flashing across, to cut off Big Dewi's head, as four others held him down, but by the time it hit him, the sword had turned into a soggy banana, which squashed harmlessly into Dewi's left ear. Then, there came a great whack – Blodwen, back in the fray, welded two Grog heads together with an almighty smash, as they tried to overcome Big Dewi with bananas. He rolled over and jumped clear.

Big Dewi batters the Grogs with a pancake mix

Again, the witch cackled, as she went into a tight 6G turn. Mr Quack, the cat, hung on grimly; such aerobatics on a draughty broomstick did not appeal. "Stand by ASBs," ordered the witch, as she roared in again from over the lake. Mr Quack primed the anti-shipping bombs.

"Fire!"

Mr Quack pressed the button, two exploding chick-peas dropped out of the bomb bay and smashed into two of the bombarding Grog boats. "He he he" The witch was enjoying this and heaved with laughter so much that her goggles misted up. More thunder-bolts shot from her wand, though her accuracy was badly affected by her poor vision. She almost

Coarsecackle hots up the action by setting Grog backsides alight

ran into a large tree, in the excitement. Most of the Grogs by now found themselves wielding bananas, and the knife in the Pontificator's belt had also been turned into a banana, giving him a strange protrusion from the left hip.

"What have you got there, then?" enquired Meinir, a strange look coming over her face, as she tried to grab his banana. The Pontificator was not amused and set off to find a quiet spot in which to try to undo the witch's erratic handiwork.

Big Dewi wondered why the witch had turned up, when she had said that she was going to a convention run by the Rhayader Witches' Institute, to be convened on a knoll above Caban Coch Reservoir. In fact, Coarsecackle had become annoyed with the bickering. After some time of squabbling amongst themselves for the best seats, she let loose some of her fiendish gooseberries, and soon cleared the meeting. This enabled her to get away early, for some more interesting activity.

The major sat open-mouthed. Out on the lake, the *Brecon Tart* and the *Strawberry Meringue* were sinking, and Ongut was once again on his way to the bottom of the lake. The witch began another fiery pass on her broomstick. As she turned on full power, she released a series of cluster-gooseberries, tiny versions that burst out of their containers above head level. Each gooseberry homed in on a Grog, and they

stuck like limpets to Grog backsides, generating incredible heat, until they smouldered alarmingly. The only course of action was to jump into the lake. Rapidly, the clearing was becoming devoid of Grogs, as they raced into the lake, with their backsides on fire.

Witch Coarsecackle sank a couple more boats, then pulled the stick back and shot up into the sky at an almost vertical angle, to Mr Quack's alarm. To those below, she was only a small speck, as she levelled off at the apex of her climb and eased back the throttle.

"Have you spotted the main fleet, yet, Quack?" she yelled, annoyed that the main Grog fleet could not be seen.

"No, I don't know where they are," came the reply, as the little cat searched the lake shore from high up.

"Right, let's give them something to remember."

With a deafening cackle, she thrust the stick forward, and, to Mr Quack's utter horror, dived straight down like a stone. As she did so, she set off the siren – a terrifying noise that sounded like a donkey braying in jerking, double-echo hoots. Coarsecackle plunged down on the last two boats of the bombarding squadron as they tried to get under way. They began zigzagging desperately, in an attempt to dodge the missiles about to descend upon them. It was to no avail: with spectacular explosions, both vessels disintegrated, as the broomstick pulled out of its dive.

Several Grogs had regrouped and were about to charge the re-formed Doddie line. The major remembered Mrs Maudlin-Grommet and waved his arm high in the air. The Grogs came forward, ready to charge, when, suddenly, to their horror, they caught sight of what appeared to be Doddie reinforcements coming from round a cliff behind the Doddie line. These looked like tall, military Doddies, with high, black helmets, red cloaks and armed with spears. After all the aerial battering from Witch Coarsecackle, this was too much, even for the warlike Grogs. They turned and fled, with Big Dewi and his friends in hot pursuit. The major chuckled, as Mrs Maudlin-Grommet marched up with her 'soldier ladies'. Their tall black hats had been mistaken for helmets and, from a distance, they appeared to be a pretty formidable force.

"I've found them," yelled Mr Quack. "The boats are under the trees in that small bay to the south."

"Wonderful," cackled the witch gleefully. "Agh-agh-agh ha! ha! Prime the Air-to-Surface Catherine-Wheels, Quack. Conventional bombs are useless for targets covered by trees"

There was hardly anything conventional about Witch Coarsecackle. She turned the broomstick into another 6G turn and headed out across the lake, before again turning to line up on the target. "Are you ready?"

"Bombs ready," answered Mr Quack.

She thrust the stick forward and they dived steeply down, then, levelled out. The broomstick was now flying in on a low-level attack. This would be tricky, as they were highly visible to the Grogs, but the witch could not see any Grogs to engage with her wand or gooseberries. Mr Quack concentrated on the bomb-sight in front of him.

"Steady," he called, "keep her steady." This would have to be a slow approach, to ensure that they hit the targets.

"Left a bit. Steady. Now, down a bit – that's fine." Arrows started to whiz past, as they came within range of the Grog archers guarding the craft.

"Damn this flak," screamed the witch, trying to keep her temper. She managed to turn some of the arrows into pancakes, but she was in danger of being overwhelmed by numbers. "Fire!"

Mr Quack pressed the bomb release just as a flying pancake hit him full square on the nose. With a distinct jerk, four Catherine-Wheels rocketed off the outer pods of the broomstick and sped horizontally towards the boats. After half a second in flight, each one ignited and tore, flaming, into the Grog fleet, which was closely gathered for defence against a Doddie attack. The whole fleet was on fire in seconds. Grogs ran for their lives.

Coarsecackle gained altitude and then flew round in a huge arc, to come in once more over Aberdod. As she came over for the final time, she did a spectacular victory roll, by far the most terrifying thing Mr Quack had ever endured. At the same time, she released a battery of fireworks, which shot high into the now-darkened sky and exploded. As they descended in a wild variety of massed colours fringed by sparklers, a star-spangled *Ddraig Goch* lit up the centre, breathing fire, as all red dragons do. With a final uproarious cackle, she roared off over the horizon, as every Doddie stood up and cheered.

But Leila and her girls had been overlooked by all this. They were still a threat and might well rally the Grog remnants that still battled on in parts of Aberdod. She paused to wipe some Doddie blood off her nose and snarled, "At 'em, girls, we've nearly finished 'em off – Gra-Gra-Grog!"

Ongut

10. Leila's Last Fling

While Leila and the Grog females attacked in the quarry, word spread up to Gladys on top of the crag. She leapt into action; calling her girls to follow, she ran into the vegetation along the ridge linking her crag with the top of the cliff, from where the Grogs abseiled. They burst through the bushes and out on to the far side, as more Grogs began abseiling.

"Into them, girls," yelled Gladys, her pole driving hard into a Grog stomach and sending the girl flying over the cliff. Only about a dozen Grogs remained at the top of the cliff, and these had been completely taken by surprise. A chaotic rough and tumble followed, with the advantage on the side of the Doddie ladies, as the Grogs had their backs to the cliff. Some slipped over before they could recover, and two decided to brave the rope rather than face these fanatical Doddie women. Gladys Price smacked one so hard across the mouth that she swallowed a large tooth, and then hopped around uncontrollably for several minutes, before disappearing into the bushes.

As Gladys fought like a tiger, Daisy managed to break through the fighting and slashed two ropes with her bread-knife, sending at least one Grog prematurely to the bottom. Despite being outnumbered, the Grogs were putting up a terrific fight, and it took Gladys, Ceinwen and Daisy together to subdue one large female, who kept snarling, until Daisy whacked her over the head with her fish-shaped bread-board and knocked her out. Two more Grogs fell over the cliff, and the Doddie girls knew it was only time before they triumphed. The last two Grogs fought like demons, until overcome by sheer numbers. Daisy despatched the last one by sticking the Grog's head into her enormous bread-bin and jamming the cover over her.

"Quite a kitchen you carry around with you, Daisy," gasped Gladys, in amazement at her friend's accessories.

"Helps pass the time, it does, when you have a few spare moments," replied Daisy, recovering her breath after such a supreme effort. "Who are those down there, Glad?" She pointed at a low hill to the north.

"Oh! It's Colonel Gnowse-Pickering's soldiers," said Gladys, recognising the Cavalry

Squadron. "They sometimes come down to Builth on manoeuvres, and water their frogs on the Groe. Wave to them – perhaps they'll finish things off for us." The girls stood up and waved, watching the cavalry charge down the hill and into the valley between them.

"Yes, there's definitely a battle taking place on that hill, sah," Lieutenant Lushuss sounded adamant. "Shall I sound the chaahge?" He checked his squadron. All were present and in order, with the two guns behind. The band had deployed beside the guns, in a prominent position, and were playing the regimental march '*A-hopping we will go.'*

The bugler sounded the charge and, gloriously, the 2nd Squadron charged into the valley, helmets gleaming, flags flying, lances tilted forward, sabres drawn and frogs hopping at full speed. Drums beat, and '*A-hopping we will go'* changed to a medley of Llandod airs, as the gun crews erected their guns, in case of attack.

With tremendous *élan*, the squadron swept down into the valley, gaining speed, all in perfect formation; and, without pause, began hopping up the far side, towards the hill where Gladys and the girls were just finishing off the last Grog. Major Berk brought the troopers to a stop just short of the Doddie ladies.

"Good afternoon, Colonel bach," said Gladys, wiping her hand on her apron.

"Major, actually," replied Major Berk, reluctantly shaking her hand without dismounting from the back of his frog. "Where's the … ? He tailed off as Gladys tugged his arm, to jerk Berk off his mount.

"Let me give you a bi-ig hug, major." She gleefully threw her arms around him and gave him a real snorter on the cheek, much to his embarrassment, in front of his men, as well. "Nice to see you. There's tidy you all look, on your lovely frogs. Thanks for coming. We've sorted out the Grogs up here."

With some difficulty, he struggled free. "Yes, quite. Now where's the enemy?"

There was a yell from the sergeant-major. "Saaaaah! Bit of bovver in progress down there, saaaaah!" He pointed further down the valley, along a route that led to the Great Clearing. One of the Grog remnant bands appeared to be fighting a pitched battle down there. "Jolly disappointing to find that the Doddie ladies have thrashed the Grogs before we arrived – perhaps we can have some real action now!".

"Sound the charge, lieutenant!"

Once more, with clockwork precision and perfect timing, every trooper hopped-off to charge back down into Cwm Coblyn, a sight Gladys and her friends will never forget. The synchronised hopping of one hundred and sixty-five frogs, charging in meticulous formation, is a truly unforgettable sight. The 2nd

The cavalry charge into Cwm Coblyn

Light Cavalry Squadron looked magnificent. Captain Squidge-Dunker, who was in charge of the artillery, gazed admiringly at the troopers, tears of pride rolling down his cheeks, as his comrades rode into battle.

Down below, the Grog remnant group had been chased up the lane by many of the regrouped Doddies, their tridents exacting a heavy toll on the Grogs' rears. This is the battle that the Light Cavalry Squadron observed from above. Few of the Grogs had any stomach for fighting any more, and many gave up, when they realised how hopeless it was for them. Most ran off into the bushes. This was the scene as the 2nd Light Cavalry Squadron swept majestically down Cwm Coblyn, filling the whole valley floor with a mass of hopping frogs, in anticipation of a tremendous battle.

On they came, to the rollicking tune of '*On Llandod Moor with Big Bertha*.' The regimental standard towered high above the centre of the charging mass, next to the gallant Major Berk, the frogs raising clouds of dust that blotted out much of the surroundings. Alas, when they reached the expected battle area, all they found were Will Pant-y-felin, Ifan Gof and a number of other Doddies tying up a few Grog prisoners. The squadron had once again been cheated of a battle.

"Good to see you, Colonel," greeted Will Pant-y-felin. "Very nice of you to come."

"Major, actually. Can you tell me where the damn enemy is?" asked the major, becoming perplexed at all this charging about to no avail. Operation *Parrot Soup* was not exactly going to plan. His answer came with a resounding crack, as the two guns opened up on the hill above. Because of the vegetation, not much could be seen from down below, but, then, a signaller ran up to the major and excitedly yelled up at him.

"Heliograph message from the gunners, sir. It says, 'Under-pants need ironing!'"

"What?" roared the major. "What impertinence! That can't be right. Check it again."

"He's repeating the message, sir." The signaller watched the mirror flashes carefully. "Ah, I see. He got it wrong first time, sir. The message reads, 'Under attack, need assistance!' It's not easy, watching him flashing in this bright sunlight, and 'attack' looks very much like 'pants' if you drop your ps."

"Hrrrruuccch! Sound the charge, Lushuss!"

Lieutenant Lushuss groaned. "Hiah we go again," he muttered under his breath. He ordered the charge, and again with great pomp, the 2nd Light Cavalry Squadron moved into action. The major directed them back up the hill to where Gladys and her girls had fought, so that they could sweep across at the enemy,

Mrs Squnch sits on a lady Grog, pinning her to the ground

which they could not even see yet. Up above, the guns were firing non-stop. Smoke drifted down the valley.

Captain Squidge-Dunker and his gun crews, on their little knoll, saw the Grogs charging towards them. These were led by the notorious Igrun, eager to capture the guns and use them against the Doddies. They turned the guns to bear on them. The first shots scattered the Grogs, but still the remainder charged on. The small infantry group slowed down the Grogs, until more grapeshot tore into them. The fight then degenerated into local tussles, with the band well into the *Ithon Waggling Song* at this point.

Major Berk rallied his squadron at the top of the hill and then, 165 troopers raced forward towards their guns. Unfortunately, as they arrived at the gun positions, they could not find one Grog left standing. All had been shot, or had run off into the bushes. For the third time, the Squadron had been robbed of a jolly good punch-up.

"We decimated them, sir, with our guns," reported Captain Squidge-Dunker cheerfully. "Blew the lot away."

The major was not impressed.

After sinking with his boat, Ongut struggled back to the shore and was recovering under some bushes with three of his crew, when two other battered-looking Grogs appeared.

"We're done for," gasped the shorter Grog. "Ongut, the military have arrived – our lads are beaten. We must flee."

"Flee, nonsense," barked Ongut, still pulling weeds and lake life out of his armour. He rose pompously to his feet. "A tactical retreat to our war-boats must be made, and then, we can regroup. Gather as many as you can and make for the boats. We'll see you there."

Without his sword, and clutching a sawn-off dandelion-stalk, Ongut looked faintly ridiculous, still dripping from his fifth ducking. He took his crew – or rather, what remained of them, along the shore, where they stumbled on a couple of Doddie coracles.

"Here they are," he said, pulling one down to the water. "I saw them under the bushes, when I swam back in. Now, pay attention: I shall only show you once how to operate these boats."

Ongut strode confidently into the shallow water, towing the coracle. He jumped into the craft, which spun out into the lake.

"You propel the boat with …" His instructions tailed off, as he realised there were no oars or paddles. In dismay, he could feel his bottom getting rather wet again. As he was facing in the wrong direction and could not see that the coracle was rapidly filling up with water through the Doddie leg-holes, he was sinking fast before he could do anything about it. The jaws of his crew dropped in synchronised amazement, as their beloved leader began to list heavily to starboard. With a gurgle, Ongut hit the bottom of the lake, his twitching head still sticking ludicrously out of the water.

His crew could hardly contain themselves, and ran for their lives, when a ferocious Ongut charged out of the water like some latter-day Poseidon, but clutching a battered dandelion stalk instead of a trident. He was last seen storming into the woods, muttering curses.

Doddies everywhere were now on the rampage. Word spread to the Great Clearing that Leila and her girls were running amok in the quarry, and so Big Dewi led a group of Doddies to join in the battle. By now, Mrs Squnch was fighting a losing battle with two Grogs: one fat lady Grog sat on top of her, whilst the other tried to shut up the old battleaxe by inserting a turnip into her large mouth. Old Elfyn had been pinned under a fallen trunk from some bush. Little Rhiannon flinched, as she underwent a battering from two attackers, while trying to hold them off with a dust-pan and brush, desperate to protect the Doddie children. The girls of St Loosenuts had run out of missiles to throw, and from high up on the quarry ledges, they were taunting the Grogs with a hastily made-up chorus of

"We hate you Grogs –
Go back to your bogs!
Hurrah, for St Loosenuts!"

The other Doddie women looked absolutely exhausted, but Martha was gallantly letting rip with a fusillade of stale rock-cakes, which certainly hurt the attacking Grogs. As Leila charged at her, Martha side-stepped, stuck out a leg, and the large Grog flew through the air, landing with a great thump, nose-first into a large bowl of lemon soufflé, delicately decorated with delightful blobs of strawberry jam, to a great cheer from the St Loosenuts' chorus.

Before she could get up, Martha was on top of Leila, thumping her hard. Leila, the supreme athlete, rolled over and, in one movement, sprang up and kicked Martha in the chest, sending her reeling across the quarry floor. Again she kicked, but this time, the games mistress grabbed her leg and pulled Leila over. They rolled together, wrestling furiously, into a swampy part of the quarry, not even stopping when they became totally immersed in muddy water.

At this moment, Dewi, Blodwen, Phergus and friends, including Lewis Lewis, who was still clad in his Clockwork Corset, arrived and began to sort out the Grog ladies. Whether it was the sight of Dewi and his friends, or the simultaneous arrival of Gladys, Ceinwen, and Daisy, with her intimidating bread-making equipment, we shall never know, but the Grogs simply fled in all directions. They were chased up and down the crags and round the quarry, but Grogs, being very athletic, were not easy to catch.

When she saw her comrades fleeing, Leila rose out of the swampy pool, like some Neanderthal creature, and waded to the bank. Martha followed but Leila turned and punched her back into the pool. Taking her opportunity, Leila ran like the wind, knocking Phergus off his feet as she charged past. Big Dewi caught sight of her and gave chase, though with little hope of catching her. Across the clearing she ran and into the vegetation beyond. Dewi followed in hot pursuit, but he quickly ran out of steam.

Dewi stopped. It was pointless chasing Leila. He recovered his breath. Suddenly, a scream of terror shattered the quiet of the woods. Again, he heard it, urgent and appealing. He ran towards the sound and, after a few moments, emerged into a clearing. Essie and two other Doddie girls, having been set free from the net, were trying to fight off Leila, but the Grog had caught Essie by the throat, to stop her screaming. The other two lay dazed on the ground.

"Come any nearer, and I'll break her neck with my bare hands," threatened Leila, as she turned towards Big Dewi. Her cruel smile convinced Dewi that it would be foolish to try anything. Leila grasped Essie's pigtails in her other hand, and strode off, dragging the girl behind her. "I swore to get my revenge on you, and so you're coming with me, little Doddie."

Dewi felt helpless and grief-stricken at the thought of losing Essie. He followed at a distance, unsure what to do. He did not have the guile of his little friend, or the speed of Martha, but whilst Leila was dragging Essie along, at least he could keep up with them.

Whenever he got too close, Leila turned and snarled at him, giving Essie a twist of the neck each time, which made her gasp in pain.

After a while, Dewi realised there was someone padding along behind him. He glanced over his shoulder and saw that it was Martha. She had heard the row and caught up with them. As he turned round, she put a finger to her lips, to keep him silent. After whispering to him, she moved to one side behind tall vegetation. Dewi challenged Leila.

"Hey, Groggie, Essie needs a rest. She's tired."

Leila stopped, turned round and laughed at Dewi. "You Doddies are so pathetic, so weak. She's coming with me." She lifted Essie with one arm and shook her like a rattle. Essie whimpered, whilst Dewi stood enraged nearby.

Suddenly, something hurtled across from the direction of Martha and caught Leila smack in the face. Before she could recover, another missile hit the Grog between the eyes. Without hesitation, Dewi leapt forward and charged head-down at Leila. His hammer-head smashed into Leila's stomach, knocking her over and releasing Essie from the vice-like grip. Leila struck out but, because she had dough over her face, she could not see. Her punching hit fresh air. Dewi grabbed her and they tumbled down a slope, scrapping as they went.

Martha sprang to her little cousin's side and

Eric the window cleaner

helped her up. They watched the other two thrashing about in the undergrowth, then, they saw Leila leap up, sprint across a grassy bank and, with a tremendous leap, dive spectacularly into the lake below. She swam across to the far headland. Dewi joined the other two, and gave Essie a long, big hug that almost squeezed all the breath out of her.

"Not so hard, Dewi," she said, "but thanks so much." He blushed like a beetroot, when she gave him a lingering kiss on the cheek.

"You're an angel."

"She's like a wild animal," said Martha, as she watched Leila swimming away, "cruel, yet amazingly agile, with the grace of a panther."

"She certainly takes some stopping," agreed Dewi. "Tell me, Martha, what did you throw at her?"

"Oh, only some dough rolls out of Daisy's bag, which I happened to be carrying for her. They wouldn't have stopped Leila, but they distracted her enough for you to get in your tackle. You certainly know how to use your head."

The three friends set off back into Aberdod, arm-in-arm, happy it was all over. The Elfael Field Force rounded up all the Grog remnants and took them away, much to the satisfaction of the Doddies, while the Prime Potcher summoned everyone to the Great Clearing, to ascertain if any were missing. Slowly, the Doddie numbers swelled. Some were limping, others aching, a number were bleeding, but most seemed to be OK, including Captain Portly-Wobble and his three companions. The remaining prisoners were released from their nets. Mr Fusspot announced with relief that, apart from much damage, all was well, and that the Orb and other Doddie treasures were safe.

No one had seen Little Dewi. Essie described how he had fallen off the raven, when they were on their way to Aberdod. Big Dewi was overcome with sadness at the disappearance of his little friend. Everyone seemed to be accounted for except Little Dewi.

"We must go and find him," said Big Dewi.

"But it's getting dark," retorted Essie, "we won't see a thing!"

"Never mind, I'll go alone," huffed back Dewi, grabbing a staff. "No-one else wants to come – I must try."

"But you can't go on your own, Dewi."

Rhiannon squeezed his arm. "I'll come with you." That did it. If little handicapped Rhiannon was going, the others could hardly opt out. Essie, Martha, Blodwen and Dai Nant-y-Cwcw joined the pair and, when Will Pant-y-felin saw them, further along, he and Gwyneth joined in.

In the dusk, they hiked up Cwm Coblyn and over the top into the next valley, following an old rabbit-run, in the direction Essie reckoned they must have flown in order to return to Aberdod. Lower down, they entered thick undergrowth, and continued to follow the rabbit-run to *Pont-y-gwiwer,* the Bridge of the Squirrel, built by the Llandoddies. This was named after a rogue squirrel that used to attack Doddies as they crossed the bridge, and the bridge was the only way to cross a deep ditch without taking a long detour. As they approached in the gloom, they could make out something moving across the bridge towards them, a hunched, dark shape that squeaked and seemed to breathe in heavy gasps. The Doddies froze, gazing wide-eyed at the bridge.

A sudden crash followed by a low howl made the group recoil in fright. The creature seemed to be rocking back and forth, as though about to charge – had it seen them?

"Aaarrrgh!" roared the creature, clearly angry.

"I know that voice – it's Eric, the window-cleaner," said Will. "What you up to, then, Eric?"

Eric looked up as the friends approached him; his cart was hanging precariously over the edge of the bridge.

"Aagh aagh – Moi cart's stucked over d'edge. Oi've bin up Rhosllanfihangel-yn-y-gors clinnin' all 'em dirty windees." Eric was not the most articulate of Doddies, but meant well. "Gimme 'and, will yer?"

The Doddies grabbed his cart and hauled it back on to the bridge. Something moaned inside. To their absolute astonishment, they saw a figure lying on his stomach inside the cart. It was Little Dewi.

"Good heavens, Dewi Bach!" yelled Wild Blod excitedly.

Little Dewi moved with obvious difficulty and could barely lift his head to see his friends. Big Dewi was beside himself with emotion.

"Aaagh aagh – Oi found 'im up a twizzle, fasted boi 'is back-soide," Eric tried to explain, but only made people even more confused.

"What's a twizzle, Eric?" demanded Essie, as Blod comforted Little Dewi.

"I think he means a thistle," said Dai, at which Eric jumped about with a grin on his face. "Dewi must have been caught up in a thistle when he fell."

"He's got a bottom bristling with thistles," said Wild Blod, extracting a yell from Little

Dewi, as she tried to pull one out. "I'll take you home, little fellow, and sort you out."

Little Dewi twisted uncomfortably at the thought of Blodwen pulling all the thistles out of his bottom – there were rather a lot.

In the dark, with only two lanterns between them, the group wound its way along the track and back to Aberdod. Eric brought his cart round to Blod's home under the roots of a willow, and they lowered Dewi onto her bed and left him to her tender care.

The next day was a dismal, wet affair, which considerably cheered up the Doddies. How they loved wet weather. They gathered in the Great Clearing. The military were to give a victory parade. All this was somewhat strange behaviour to the laid-back Doddies, but it was good entertainment, especially when the band began playing. The Grand Lurbe of Doddies was there, with his wife, Lurbess Hyacinth, and their five appalling children, plus the Prime Potcher, Grand Pontificator and other Doddie Notables, and several high-ranking officials from the Twerpanis, to celebrate their deliverance. Even Haydn the Hermit turned up on one of his rare visits, to see how the Doddies had fared. Mrs Maudlin-Grommet, Sidney and their brood sat nearby, Mrs M a little put out because she wasn't sitting on the stage with the Notables.

Colonel Gnowse-Pickering, sitting stiffly on

the blackest frog Big Dewi had ever seen, led the procession. He was followed by the band, the 2nd Light Cavalry Squadron and the artillery battery, all looking splendid, even in the drizzle now descending. The colonel saluted as he passed the stage, and the procession formed up behind him in the Great Clearing. He was invited on to the stage by the Twerpanis, where he was awarded the Purple Sprout, their highest medal for bravery in combat.

As the medal was being pinned to the colonel's chest, Big Dewi couldn't resist the urge to comment in a very loud voice, "What's he got that for, then? He's not done anything. He just sat on his backside, back at head-quarters."

"Ssshh, Dewi," said Will. "That's how it works, see. The highest awards always go to those who don't really deserve them, because of who they know, not what they actually do."

"I think he's got a cheek," commented Essie. "He only sent the soldiers when he thought he wouldn't get any more cakes! Dewi Mawr is the real hero."

At this point, while the colonel saluted after receiving his medal, there was a sudden flash of lightning. The expectant crowd hushed, the dark clouds parted and out roared the unmistakeable sight of Witch Coarsecackle on her Sky Scimitar II broomstick, accompanied by the faithful Quack and followed in line astern by Zephyrs 1, 2 and 3.

"Agh – agh – agh –ha! ha! ha!" came the insane cackle, and as the witch zoomed over the clearing, her wand flashed. Every Doddie mouth was agape, as the colonel, at his most glorious moment of pomp, saw his medal turned into a large stick of glo-brite rhubarb that pulsed like a fairy candle, and, at the same time, his trousers fell down. Before Colonel Gnowse-Pickering could recover from this display of classic Coarsecackle spomduffery, Zephyr One let fly with a great dollop of slug-flavoured bird-shit, which caught the colonel squarely on the nose. This was repeated by an even moister sample from Zephyr Two. Zephyr Three, however, a bird currently in training, had targeting problems, and as she was about to let fly, she aborted and circled overhead. The colonel, clearing muck from his vision, watched the raven come in again on a bombing run. He jumped off the stage and ran, zigzagging and trouser-less, across the clearing, towards his troopers, pursued by the playful Zephyr Three. Again, the bird overshot without releasing its load. The breathless colonel paused, and warily watched the bird circle round and turn towards him again. The crowd, including the troopers, fell about in hysterical laughter as Zephyr Three finally delivered her moist payload. It caught the colonel on his left cheek, and left his large moustache dripping with the foul-smelling stuff.

Big Dewi rocked with laughter, glad that pompous old Gnowse-Pickering had been cut down to size. As she flashed by for an encore, the crowd rose to Coarsecackle and spontaneously sang out 'For she's a jolly good Doddie!' till they were hoarse.

Little Dewi came out, with the help of Wild Blod and Rhiannon, and joined in the festivities for St Cewydd's Day. Even though it was 24 hours late this time, the event was celebrated as wildly as ever. Only, this time, the assembled Doddies were thankful that the Pontificator had not had the opportunity to give another of his dreadful speeches.

As Dewi started gobbling down a piece of jam sponge, he saw Mrs Maudlin-Grommet striding purposefully towards him, her severe jaw betraying strong determination.

"Dewi Mawr!" she exclaimed, and flung her arms around him, as he started to back off. A wild look came over his face, as he realised she might be about to kiss him. Mrs Maudlin-Grommet had never been known to kiss anyone before. He struggled, but her very wet kiss fell on his huge nose, at the same time as the remains of his jam sponge were accidentally stuffed into his left ear.

"Dewi," she said, you saved my dear Sidney."

No one had ever seen her so emotional, and Big Dewi was taken aback.

"Right, my lovely," Blod directed her remarks at Dewi, as she sidled up to him, "now it's my turn. I want to look at all your wounds, butty, and get you all tidy-like, see."

"Oh, no, Blod. You won't find any marks on me, girl." By now Dewi was pretty unnerved by all this female attention.

Blodwen seemed determined and Dewi could not see a way out of the predicament. Suddenly, he was swept up by the grateful Doddies, and carried shoulder-high out of the clutches of Wild Blodwen, to be fêted by the crowd.

Old Shemmy Jones had had a great day in the Llanerch Inn. All afternoon, they'd been singing raucously at his mate's funeral wake, the songs getting wilder and ruder as the afternoon progressed. At eight-thirty, he was slung out for being too drunk, and so he staggered erratically back home, still singing loudly. As he passed by Llandrindod Lake, he was amazed to see a mess of rubbish floating about near the shore. "Them damn ducks," he muttered. As he looked, he suddenly made out a tiny coracle with two little figures in it, the size of his thumb. He watched them float out into the lake then, excitedly, he searched for a long stick, to try to push them in towards the shore. Alas, when he turned back to catch the coracle, it had vanished into thin air.

Dr Phatbellie

Doddie Words & Sayings

Clagged his faffer – gone barmy, derived from the blocking of the faffer valve on a snurting-bag

Faffing-valve – part of the snurting-bag that allows it to be played underwater

Fish-sponger – bag for carrying fish, among other things

Ibgur – Doddie game similar to rugby, played by both males and females

Krapolian saddle – large double-saddle with bars for security used by Krapol warriors who live in the Cambrian mountains

Phyrgian Thunderbolt – particularly destructive thunderbolt that turns things into a bubbling red mass of lava, generally only found in the land of Phyrgia

Prut – plant sensitive to air pressure, which changes colour, size, smell and emits grunts

Qork – a type of horned slug with magical properties understood by very few

Snufter – similar to a fire brigade, only responds to wild animals penetrating the village by blowing a kind of snuff at them

Squirt-bags – used to spray foul-smelling fumes to repel aggressive wildlife

Squrt – Doddie money

Snurting – playing the underwater snurting-bag – like bagpipes

Spomduffery – mayhem caused when magic spells get out of control

Spondean Carp – large fish with low IQ, found in the lakes of Spondea

Stunker – important position in the ibgur team

Griswallt ap Llechitwyt is alarmed at the popularity of Erwood Craft Centre, as he prefers to avoid the crowds when sipping afternoon tea at his favourite watering hole.

Llandeilo Graban, Builth Wells, Powys, LD2 3SJ
Open February–December 10.00–18.00
www.erwood-station.co.uk

Llandrindod Wells Spa Town Trust

- Farmers' Market
- Health Centre
- Summer Soaker
- Heritage Centre

www.llandrindod.co.uk

MID WALES JOURNAL

To keep an eye on Grumpie affairs the Llandoddies sneak into the offices of the **Mid Wales Journal** on the night before publication. It takes four Doddies to hold, read and note down the contents of their favourite paper.

Why is Llandrindod Post Office so popular?

Come along and find out!

For a full list of books currently in print,
send now for your free copy
of our full-colour catalogue
— or simply surf into our website

www.ylolfa.com

for secure on-line ordering.

TALYBONT CEREDIGION CYMRU SY24 5AP
e-bost ylolfa@ylolfa.com
gwefan www.ylolfa.com
ffôn (01970) 832 304
ffacs 832 782